DISCOUNT PRICE

A Friend of Mary Rose

BOOKS BY ELIZABETH FENWICK

A Friend of Mary Rose

A Long Way Down

Poor Harriet

A Friend of Mary Rose

by Elizabeth Fenwick

Harper & Brothers • Publishers • New York

A FRIEND OF MARY ROSE. Copyright © 1961 by Elizabeth Fenwick Way. Printed in the United States of America. All rights reserved. No part of the book may be used or reproduced in any manner whatsoever without written permission except in the case of brief quotations embodied in critical articles and reviews. For information address Harper & Brothers, 49 East 33rd Street, New York 16, N.Y. Library of Congress catalog card number: 61-17559.   I-L

A Friend of Mary Rose

Chapter One

On the day they were to move, Mr. Nicholas rose in darkness at his usual hour. An unacceptably early hour, he knew, to the adolescents and middle-aged adults with whom he lived; but rather late for his cat.

This cat, an illegal companion at night, started Mr. Nicholas off every day with the same problem: to get it downstairs undiscovered. It was a wretched cat, as a co-conspirator, and moreover very lively and hungry at this hour. It would not let itself be caught and carried down. So the moment he opened his door he had to be ready to follow, and follow fast—the slightest pause meant yowls, and yowls meant the end of his game. For Mr. Nicholas had his scruples. He would not have taken the cat up at night with him, if she had actually told him not to. And as soon as she knew, she would of course tell him not to.

Fortunately, they were all heavy sleepers. But this morning, as soon as he opened his door, he heard his daughter-in-law's voice. Awake already! Behind the closed bedroom door her quick voice was already talking,

talking—talking his poor son out of sleep, no doubt. Mr. Nicholas, who had been waking to silence and solitude for years now (until he thought of the cat), listened sardonically a moment. That moment was too long; the cat cried out to hurry him.

In the deep quiet of the upstairs hall, the cry sounded incredibly loud. Providentially, the cat pressed against his leg just then, and he gave a half-shove, half-kick, that knocked it down some of the steps. He followed as rapidly as he could. It kept going, luckily. The next cry came from the kitchen door, and that was all right. They were both downstairs now, both in the kitchen. Nothing could be proved, they had won again.

His satisfaction, as he groped for its can of food (the cat loudly, legally crying at him now), was as solid as ever. His day had begun once more with purpose, with achievement, and he was not ashamed of its nature. At eighty-three, you made your life out of whatever you could, or had none.

She came in on them while he was hunting his own breakfast. At once—nervous and patient—her voice began to pour over him.

"Now, Father—what are you looking for in there? You know there's nothing—look out for those bottles! I don't know what they're doing in there, Alan was supposed to take them all back yesterday. . . . What *is* it, dear?"

"I can't find my bananas," he said. When she gave him the chance.

"Well, they wouldn't be in there!"

A Friend of Mary Rose

He said nothing, while she rummaged.

"Well, there were two left. I put them aside specially. You *sure* you didn't eat them, Father?"

He never answered nonsense of this sort. He began in silence to leave the kitchen. There were no bananas.

"I suppose the children got them, then . . . though they know perfectly well they're not to eat the last ones, ever. I'll have to make you something," she said, resigned. "What would you like, dear?"

A martyr already, and not even six o'clock.

"Never mind," he said.

"Or if you want to wait I'll send one of the children down to the store. Would you rather do that?"

"All right. Don't fuss."

A last word like that she wouldn't let him have. Her anxious voice followed him away: "It's true I've been letting things run out, but they know they're never to touch the last of the bananas, I just can't believe they . . ."

Sounds echoed, with curtains down and rugs up. He was aware of his own quiet footfalls, the regular descent of his rubber-tipped stick, and overhead he could hear— heavy and slow—the tread of his son getting dressed. Plunk plunk. Plunk plunk plunk plunk plunk. Plunk. No other sounds than these—certainly none of children. There were no more children here, not what Mr. Nicholas called children—that woke with the light and came welcome into his room. No more of those; they were gone. And the big strangers in their beds would sleep till they were shaken out of sleep, meeting morning as late as possible, like an outrage. He would wait a long time for his bananas, if he waited for children to bring them.

He had no such idiot intention. Unbolting the front door, he went out onto the porch. The morning was freshly cool, light air from the southwest moved upon his skin. She was not going to have a rainy moving day after all, poor Martyr, she would have to make do with other, smaller grievances. Well, he would help her along, he would start her out right, if she would just give him time to get going.

Sometimes she had an intuition that dismayed him, and when at last—beyond the gate, the gate quietly shut behind him—he found himself on his way, he was surprised at his luck. Or at her failure in vigilance. He set a safe boundary for himself, beyond which he could pretend not to hear her, and reached that, too: the swollen part of the sidewalk where the great tree root had wrenched it up, in front of Thompsons'.

He was now out of her territory, in public domain. And he was going to fetch his bananas for himself.

From the curtainless hall window, Dorothea Nicholas watched him go. He was past the worst spot; the rest of the way was clear—or should be clear, at this hour. Unless some child had left a tricycle or a wagon out overnight, for him to fall over and fracture his poor old bones, and be bedridden from then on. . . . Her tic jumped; she put an absent, gentle finger on it, and then stepped out onto the porch. From here she could see the sidewalk all the way to the corner, where the little grocery store

A Friend of Mary Rose

was, and it was clear. Besides, he was using his stick very carefully, ahead of himself.

She let him go. This was his last morning in his old home; she would let him have his adventure, and go up to the store for himself. It couldn't set any precedent.

Standing there a moment longer, consciously indulgent, she continued to examine the street that she was leaving. It was years since she had seen it so empty, so clear of people. So *clean* of people. It seemed almost itself again, the way she had first known it twenty years ago when she had come here as Johnny's bride, to visit his parents. Even then it had been going down, and the big clapboard and shingle houses had been a bit shabby; but most of the yards were kept up, most of the old owners still lived there. Now this early look of emptiness restored much of its old dignity. Because *people* were what had ruined DeKuyper Street—too many people, more and more of them crowding in as the old houses changed hands, the houses that were too big for single families nowadays. Or too big for the kind of families that came to live on DeKuyper Street. Apartments and rooms, makeshift apartments and furnished rooms, had multiplied all round; and the people who rented them had multiplied, too. They were transient people, not many stayed long enough to seem familiar, but they seemed to replace each other by some inexorable law of progression—two for one, four for two—until sometimes Dorothea was haunted by wonder at where and how they all must sleep. Children in cellars? In closets without windows, in beds with too many other children or adults? There was no way to know, they were all strangers. Except for old Mrs. Thompson next door (desolate at their leaving), and the Rudds with their corner store—and the Haydens going to wrack and ruin at the other end of the block—she no longer knew anyone at all. Well, it was time—past time—to be moving away. She was moved by this last, familiar view of the street where she had lived for nearly ten years, but it did not change her mind in the least. She was glad, relieved, to be going from it at last. If only the moving were over . . .

She gave a last, resigned look at her father-in-law's progress—he was almost there—and then went inside.

Immediately, as if safety had abandoned him with her leaving, she thought of the store being shut. It never seemed to be—early, late, Sundays, holidays, one or both of the Rudds always seemed to be there. To be open was their main commodity, in fact, and allowed them to survive along with the big chain stores that offered more, and cheaper, but not always. Six o'clock, though . . . she had never tried them this early.

The telephone was still connected (because of Father, in the night), and she rang the corner store and got Mrs. Rudd on the second ring.

Cordial with relief, she said: "It's Mrs. Nicholas, Mrs. Rudd. I just wanted to be sure you're open this early. . . ."

"Oh, yes, we're open, Mrs. Nicholas. My, *you're* getting an early start today, aren't you?"

"Yes. . . . What I called you for is that Father's on his way down, and I wanted to be sure you were open."

"Oh, is that right? Well, bless his heart, I'll surely look out for him. . . . Oh, here he is now," she said, dropping her voice, although the telephone was at the back of the store. "I can see him coming up the step right now—my, he certainly gets around well for a blind man his age. But don't you think somebody'd better see him home, Mrs. Nicholas? Should I keep him here awhile, till you can send for him?"

Dorothea had been reminding herself for ten years that Mrs. Rudd's effusive barbs were not intentional, just tactless. At this last moment, she allowed herself a different judgment.

"I'm afraid he might not like that, Mrs. Rudd. I'm sure he'll be all right. But thank you just the same."

She also allowed herself a little grimace, hanging up. Her husband, coming downstairs, caught her at it.

"Who was that?"

He was a big man, like his father, but like him in no other way. Just as well; the house would never have held two of them. She looked at him with automatic anxiety.

"Where did you get that tie? That's not the one I left out."

"Yes, it is," he said, surprised.

Was it? Momentary uncertainty invaded Dorothea. First the bananas, now the tie . . . she really *didn't* remember, about either one!

Her husband came up and put his hand on her shoulder.

"Now, take it easy, hon—you're almost through. Easy does it."

Elizabeth Fenwick

It didn't, of course. She replied, in oblique dissent, "I was talking to Mrs. Rudd—Father's gone down there alone, I wanted to be sure she was open."

"What did he do that for?"

"There were no bananas. He didn't want to wait, or have anything else."

"Oh, Lord," he said, to her tone more than to her words.

He followed her out to the kitchen. The cat was licking itself on the table; he managed to push it off before she saw.

"I better go get him," he said.

"No, let him alone."

He went on watching her uncertainly, as she started his breakfast.

"Look, Dot—why don't I take him with me today? I don't know why we never thought of this, you shouldn't have him all day when you're moving. When you don't even want me around," he said, half joking.

"I have thought of it. They can put his rocker in last and take it out first, that's all. He can stay out on the porch here, and in the patio at the new house. It's a nice day."

"In the rocker, all day?"

"Well, he'll just have to," she said doggedly. "He couldn't stand a whole day downtown with you, he'd be worn out. And so would you," she added, in a rare escape of opinion.

He didn't say anything; but before long he got up and went out, muttering something about going to meet the

16

old boy. By then, she was glad to have him go. Mrs. Rudd would think Johnny had overruled her, but that didn't matter compared to the chance that Father might hurt himself on the way home. She had visions of an ambulance and the movers arriving simultaneously, made herself stop, and went upstairs to wake the children.

That, and breakfast, occupied her mind entirely for some time. Nearly an hour passed before she noticed that neither Johnny nor his father had come back. Then, in a panic, she fled out to the porch.

The old man was sitting there in his rocker, holding two banana skins neatly folded. Breathing hard, she took them from his hand.

"Where's John, Father?"

"Still next door, I suppose. Dorothea, about my trunks—"

"They're all ready, everything's all ready," she murmured, and escaped back into the house. "Next door" must mean Mrs. Thompson; they didn't know the other side. But what was he doing over there so long?

She had to wait nearly a half hour longer to find out; and then she could hardly believe her ears. And Johnny looked so pleased with himself! Standing there explaining to her how Mrs. Thompson—a widow not much younger than Father himself—would be delighted to have her old neighbor spend his last day in the neighborhood with her, only wished she had dared suggest it herself!

"You mean you *asked* her to keep Father today? Oh, Johnny—no!"

"Well, why not? She was glad to be asked, Dottie—I

Elizabeth Fenwick

just wish we'd asked her some other favor, all these years. You should have seen how pleased she was."

For Johnny, this was sharp, since Dorothea admittedly couldn't ask favors—though she would go to any trouble to grant them. The original do-it-yourself kid, Johnny said, joking. But he wasn't joking now.

Bewildered, even hurt, Dorothea began to put his breakfast on the table. He stopped her serving hand with his.

"Now, come on—aren't you really a little bit glad? And you don't even have to tell him, I will."

But that was too much. She found her tongue again.

"No, I will—you'll do it wrong. You'll hurt his feelings," she said unsteadily; and as if he had already done so, she left him without another word and went out to the porch.

18

Chapter Two

Mr. Nicholas was considerably startled.

That the Martyr should under any circumstances lay down any part of her load—or even let it be wrested from her—was enough to shake a man's faith in the laws of nature. Was she going to become a New Woman, in her New House? Was he going to get a New Opponent, flexible and wily, in place of his poor old Martyr?

"Hope springs eternal," he murmured.

But of course she was still there.

"Now, Father, what do you mean by that? No one is hoping anything, we just want you to be comfortable. . . ."

Suddenly inspired, he lied calmly.

"No, Dorothea—what amuses me is that I hesitated to suggest this very idea myself, because I know how much you dislike asking favors. And now you've gone and done it for yourself."

He knew quite well it was Johnny who had asked. She must know he did. Was she going to admit it?

Elizabeth Fenwick

Was she even there?

He put out his hand, touched her dress, and withdrew at once. Discovered, she said: "Be a good boy now, won't you, dear?"

"Exemplary. But about my trunks, now, Dorothea—"
She was already inside the door.

The morning life of his house went audibly on, for the last time. The Girl came crashing downstairs again, and then the Boy. Presently they would come out on the porch, approximately together, and he would get dutiful light bumps on the head as they went by; these were kisses. On clear mornings he could hear them as far as Haydens', at the corner. If they were speaking. The Girl walked like Dorothea—a lighter echo. The Boy still didn't walk, he loped, or dragged. Usually Johnny's car had come out of the driveway a good half hour before, but this morning he left late, and came out the front way—even sitting on the porch railings near his father for a little while. He didn't want to go at all; Mr. Nicholas had an ironic impulse to invite him next door, too.

After that, there was no one of his family left to listen to but the Martyr; and it often surprised him that he continued to hear and define, day after day, movements that had long since lost all capacity to surprise. In the new house, of course, he would have an immense amount of relearning to do, and he firmly considered that this would be stimulating. He knew that he still kept reserves of energy far beyond what were needed here, in this familiar routine. There was, God knew, plenty of troublesome life in him yet. At the same time, he did not want to leave.

A Friend of Mary Rose

Something approaching panic overcame him at times, to his bewilderment and shame. It was entirely irrational, and he was well able to control it, fortunately. Just as he was able to control the depression, equally irrational, which was settling on him now. Because they were farming him out next door.

Not that he minded spending a day with Lettie Thompson, who had always found him sufficiently intimidating to make her behave. She had been a good cook, too, and kept a comfortable house. No, it was a good enough idea—if only he had thought of it for himself! If only it had been he who had gone to Dorothea and said: "Now my dear, I want no part of all this hoo-ha today, and I am going over to Lettie Thompson's until you have finished with it." How upset she would have been, how full of protest! It would never have occurred to her that he might plan to leave her for a whole day, of his own volition. And of course he had not. It was she who was leaving him.

Mr. Nicholas felt for his stick, and pushed himself up. He had had enough of this maudlin trap his thoughts were in. It was time to move around. And once on his feet, he knew where he would go: to Lettie's. Belated initiative, but better than none. Dorothea would see, at least, that he liked the idea very much—that ought to dismay her.

The Thompsons' front walk gave him a little trouble; she evidently didn't keep it up in her widowhood. But he was perfectly composed by the time she opened her door.

"Well, Lettie my dear," he began—but she was too excited to hear any more, seizing his arm and almost pulling him inside, bursting all over him with speech. Poor lonely soul.

"Oh, John, I could hardly believe it when Johnny told me, I was sure he'd done it without Dorothea knowing, and she'd never let you—I told him, I said Johnny, now, don't get me into trouble, darling, you know I've been so careful all these years, girls are so touchy, and Dorothea's always so careful of him, she won't—"

"Nonsense, Lettie, nonsense." But in increasing good humor (and considerable discomfort) he let himself be hauled and bumped along through the house—where on earth were they going? He couldn't match his memory yet to this rough journey. "She's afraid I'll come courting you, that's all," he said, trying to get free—and was astonished at the sudden release and silence that followed. Why, she was taking him seriously! "She's a very sharp girl, Dorothea," he added, delighted.

But Lettie had got hold of herself and said, "Nonsense," in her turn. "Old people like us, John—shame on you!"

He wouldn't hear of being ashamed. Nothing more natural, a pretty widow next door (Was it the kitchen? It *smelled* like the kitchen)—bound to occur to any man, even an old crock like himself. (It was the kitchen; she had him down at the table of course. Lettie always fed people instantly.)

But he had gone too far, and spoiled the fun—she turned sad on him. He oughtn't to talk about himself like that, she said, it really hurt her. If he meant his sight, why, a person would hardly notice, the way he had

A Friend of Mary Rose

learned to manage. And it was really very wrong of poor Dorothea, if she had made him feel . . .

"Oh, bother my eyes," he said, tired of it. "It's my legs I want back. Legs are the thing, Lettie—hang on to your legs, and you hang on to your independence. How are yours, by the way?"

She had varicose veins, of long standing, and after a little struggle couldn't resist talking about them. He got her back to earth nicely in this way, and by eating bits of whatever she gave him; and then the movers came, and they both limped out on her porch. He settled to see the whole thing through Lettie's eyes and memories, perhaps the best way.

Also, he could find out about his trunks.

"Now they'll either be first or last," he instructed her, as she settled beside him. "The attic, you know. They haven't got an attic in this confounded new place, and I know for a fact she's putting some things in the storage warehouse. For a time, she says. I've told her I need those trunks—there isn't a week goes by I don't have one or the other of them open; but she's never given me a straight answer about it yet. You just watch, and tell me what things go with them."

Lettie promised she would. But as the moving progressed, he began to suspect that her eyes weren't much to boast about either. Besides, she got wrapped up in some piece that she either hadn't seen before or else hadn't seen in "years and years," and by the time she finished exclaiming and chattering about it they could have moved a couple of rooms past without her noticing. It didn't help to be sharp with her. If he interrupted, insisting on knowing what had just gone into the van, she always said it was a chair. He began to lose his temper.

"Don't tell me such stuff, Lettie Thompson! Why, that thing weighed a ton, it took three men—"

"It—it was a *big* chair, John. . . ."

"There isn't a chair like that in the house," he said coldly. For a time, then, she really tried to pay attention.

But to give Lettie credit, it was she who finally enlightened him. After everything was over, and Dorothea had gone off with his poor cat in its basket ("Butter its paws," he reminded her. "The minute you get there, now!")—when they were left alone to talk it over, and Lettie was still insisting that his trunks had gone in, she added thoughtfully: "But I'll tell you what I didn't see, John, and I was particularly looking out for it, and that was Mary's dining-room suite. Now I always admired that fumed oak, and there must have been at least fifteen pieces to it—"

"Twelve chairs," he said.

"That's right, and the table, and the sideboard, and the china cabinet. Why, I couldn't have missed all that! And I didn't see it. Are you sure she's taking it with her?"

"Taking it with her! What else would she do?"

"She might be putting it in storage," Lettie suggested. "She might not think it would go with a modern house. Or maybe she's leaving some of the heavy old things there—to sell, you know, or for the Salvation Army, even. You don't realize what the children think about our

A Friend of Mary Rose

furniture, John. Why, when I tried to give Carol my curly-maple bedroom—"

"Dorothea's not Carol," he said shortly. "She's not a fool, either—give it to the Salvation Army! Why, that's good, solid, valuable furniture! You couldn't buy anything like it today!"

"Well, I know that," said Lettie stubbornly. "But the point is, nobody wants to. They think our furniture is *funny*. If Dorothea were your own daughter, you'd know."

"Dorothea is my own daughter. And she asked me when she wanted to change the living room," he added, triumphant. "When she got that couch and put the settee in the attic."

"I didn't see the settee either," said Lettie.

He reached for his stick, and began to struggle up from his chair.

"Well, we'll soon settle it," he said. "Come on—I've still got my key."

"Why, John—I don't think we ought to go in there," she protested. She was struggling up, too, but only to hang on to him. "Now please, dear—I might have been mistaken, I think I was—"

"That is still my house," he said, "and I told you, I have my key."

"But Dorothea wouldn't want you wandering round like this, John—please don't, you don't need to—when you get to the new house tonight, you—"

"When I get to the new house," he said, "I want to know what I'm talking about. Oh, stay there, Lettie—I'll

25

be right back. You don't need to watch me every minute, do you?"

Apparently she felt that she did. Why, if anything should happen to him over there, if those men had left boards and nails and things lying around, and he hurt himself . . . The end of it was that he had to take her. And she had to come. It was an arrangement that pleased neither of them; but once started, they both made the best of it.

She was incredibly slow. Actually, once he was up, he could cover the ground much faster than she. Probably that was why she hadn't wanted to go—didn't want him to know how bad her legs really were. In order not to embarrass her, he had to pretend to be slow, too, and then she insisted on pointing out every pebble on her wretched path, and altogether it was a most exasperating journey.

But he had been right to insist. The dining-room furniture was still there.

He didn't need Lettie's eyes to assure him of it. His own hands, trembling with shock, with disbelief, traced out for him every familiar piece. Displaced, yes—shoved back. But all there. At last, too shaken to speak, he sank down in his old armchair. Lettie, seated long ago, sounded on the verge of tears.

"Don't take it so hard, dear—I know Dorothea will be able to, will tell you—"

"She's getting rid of everything today, isn't she?" he said, with a laugh that came out like a croak.

"Oh, John—oh, my dear old friend—"

A Friend of Mary Rose

This was intolerable. He pushed himself up again, and went over to her.

"Now stop that, Lettie. Pull yourself together, and let's go see what else she's left. Why, I could probably move right back in here," he said with iron gaiety, "and hardly miss a thing! Come on."

They toured the downstairs, Lettie frankly leaning on him. To her obvious relief, there was nothing else left behind except an old kitchen cabinet which she declared to be a wreck, just a wreck. He paid no attention to her, and investigated every bit of space himself. She was telling him the truth. But there was no reassurance for him in that.

"Come on," he said finally. "The real story will be up in the attic. I don't care too much about the settee, I suppose, but if she's left my trunks up there . . ."

"John, she wouldn't do that! All your things!"

"My things have no value for her," he said, tasting his bitterness. Chewing it. "She's made that clear. Come on."

"I can't," Lettie confessed then. "I'm sorry, but—I can't."

"What do you mean, you can't? Just take hold of my arm, and hold the rail on the other side—we'll do it slowly!"

"No," she said. "I don't do stairs any more, John. Not even at home. I could, but the doctor doesn't want me to. He's very firm about it."

"Oh," he said. Her embarrassment, and the pity of understanding, gave him pause. "No more stairs, eh?"

"No. I don't mind—the children have put in a nice bathroom downstairs, and I've made the dining room into a lovely sleeping room, but—I just can't go up, John."

"Well," he said, depressed for her (and it probably meant heart, too, poor old soul), "well, never mind. You go sit in one of my twelve chairs, Lettie, and have a rest. I'm up there all the time alone, you just sit down and wait, and I'll be right back."

But she wouldn't agree. She wouldn't let him go. Physically—and it came to that—she wouldn't let him go up.

"Why, it's my own house!" he said, growing angry. "What's the matter with you? I go over it every day of my life, I know every inch of it as well as I know my own foot! Don't be so silly, I'm ashamed of you!"

"I can't help it," she said, close to tears. "I won't let you go up there alone! Don't you understand, I couldn't reach you if something happened? I wouldn't even know! I couldn't get up all those stairs if my life depended on it," she burst out. "There! Now, that's the truth, and I don't care—and *you can't go!*"

He accepted defeat. After a moment (remembering that probable heart) he put his arm round her.

"All right. All right, Lettie—my goodness. Calm down, it's all right."

But she was really crying by then, and he led her back to the dining room and made her sit down before he would let her take him back home.

By then she was calmer, but worn out. He had no trouble persuading her to lie down for a while. She didn't even have the energy to make him stretch out on the day bed, when he claimed that he took his own naps sitting up. With no more than an afghan dropped over his knees, she dragged away, to her converted dining room–bedroom.

He heard her shut the door. He meant to allow her five or ten minutes to drop off, more than enough. Then, unencumbered, he would go back to his house and find out the truth about his trunks.

Chapter Three

It was after six o'clock when Johnny came back to DeKuyper Street. After one look at his father's face, he apologized for being so late. The movers were still unloading, he said, and Dorothea hadn't been able to get away—she just had to wait till he came home. Johnny hoped they weren't too tired, waiting.

"We're not tired at all, darling," said Mrs. Thompson brightly. "We had a wonderful morning, watching everything, and then we had some lunch, and just slept for hours. Didn't we, John?"

His father said nothing. Mrs. Thompson didn't seem to notice.

"In fact, I haven't had such a long nap in years," she went on gaily. "You can imagine how I felt, when I woke up and saw how late it was, and thought of your poor father sitting out here wondering where his hostess was! And then I came rushing out, and here he was, fast asleep, too! Imagine."

A Friend of Mary Rose

"But I'm sure they're safe, that's something quite different from old furniture. Besides, didn't you—surely you didn't leave anything . . . valuable in them, did you? I mean, for the moving?"

"They're locked," he replied absently.

"Oh, but John—*trunk* keys! Oh, dear, you mean you *did* leave money in them? You really did?"

He lifted his head in surprise.

"Money? What are you talking about, Lettie? I don't keep money in trunks, for pity's sake." She continued to sound very agitated, but made no reply, which was strange. "Why would I do that? Whatever put such an idea in your head?"

"Why—why, I don't see why you shouldn't," she said then, stammering a little. "When it's not possible to go to the bank any longer—and of course you wouldn't want to leave it just lying round in your room, with—with children in your house. I don't see anything very wrong about that. . . ."

"Well, I do," he said, sobered. "I hope you're not doing anything so foolish. You're not, are you?"

"Oh, no," she said quickly. "Everyone knows I don't keep any money here at all—everything's charged, you know, and then the bills go to George, and he handles everything. Even the paper boy, and the man who does the yard and shovels the snow. Oh, I'm very careful, John. But of course it's different for you," she added. "You're a man, and you don't live alone, and—and I think it's quite all right. Even Mrs.—"

She stopped.

"Well, Mrs. Ryan, who cleans for me—the only thing she thought was that, if there was a fire . . . Of course, even to her, I said I didn't believe a word of it. Naturally."

"Well!" he said. "Well, I'm much obliged to you, Lettie. To think I've been a famous miser all the while and didn't even know it."

"Why, that's not being a miser, nobody thinks you—"

"Certainly it's being a miser," he said. "There's no other word for a habitual money-hider that I know of." She was uneasily silent. He began to be curious. "But how did this ever start?" he wondered. "Why? I'm not a rich man, I never have been. Do I just *seem* like an old miser, nowadays? Is that it? Have I grown so unpleasant as that?"

"Oh, John—"

"No, no—that's fishing, isn't it? I'm sorry, I take it back. But how amazing . . ."

They sat in silence, until she murmured: "I think it's just that you're so independent, John. I think that's it."

He gave a short laugh.

"Well, if I am, it's not because I hide money in trunks. What a deduction! No, no—I don't mean you, Lettie, I know you've only listened to this nonsense. But it's a sad light on what our poor old street has come to. Or our poor old world, maybe." She sighed; and he changed his tone. "No, Lettie, let me assure you that I have no financial secrets from my son. And I'd be very much surprised if he has any from Dorothea. As for independence," he said steadily, "I'm entirely dependent on my son and daughter in many important ways—the fact that I have a small amount of property doesn't obscure that fact to me. Or to them, naturally."

He was not aware of having formed such a thought before, in all the years of his growing dependence, and he found it curiously satisfying. In some way, it seemed to balance the business of Dorothea and the dining-room furniture—or perhaps to diminish it. Not, however, that he didn't intend to have that out.

But he could tell from Lettie's breathing that it was time to change the subject, and so he began to tell her about his real trunks: not the money-laden ones, but the old steamer that had been Mary's and still held many of her things, and his own sturdy wooden trunk which no moth had ever invaded. Dorothea did not trust it, and always managed to seal away his overcoat and heavy suit in some contraption of her own; but he had kept his woolly blue tam-o'-shanter, for example, quite safely in that trunk ever since he bought it in Scotland, and expected it to outlast him. Without stinking of chemicals, either.

"I always know it's really winter, when I see you wearing your tam the first time," Lettie said. "Oh, dear—I will miss you, John."

"Do you remember Mary's lace collection?" he went on. "I believe you had some of it, before I put it away, didn't you? Now Dorothea really values that," he said, struck by the recollection. "I remember she was upset by the idea that you were going to put it on things and use it—as you ought to, of course. She wanted me to let her rewrap it in some kind of stuff I couldn't get open. But of course I keep it as Mary had it—she knew perfectly well how to care for her lace. Dorothea did value that," he said again. "Even though she wouldn't have any. She wouldn't have forgotten it was there."

"I'm sure your trunks are all right," Lettie replied.

It was like going through the trunks themselves, and not alone, to sit here dredging up one by one their recollected contents. He began to be sorry that Lettie had not been able to come up to the attic with him in fact; they could have spent a very pleasant afternoon, and perhaps she would have liked some other of Mary's things, or even of his. The bits of scrimshaw, for instance. He told her about these, too, and how he had come to have them— the great-aunt in Stonington, Connecticut, who had made him a present of a piece every birthday instead of leaving them to him as a collection. She had hoped he would feel, in this way, that he was making his own collection—and so he had.

It was in Mystic, near by, that he had met Mary for the first time. Lettie did not know this story, and he told it to her; and then he listened patiently to hear of her own first meeting with poor Thompson—a reedy, nervous fellow who had given up before he was sixty. She cried a little, and he helped her past it.

Altogether, the evening turned into quite a pleasant one, and he lost all sense of wishing it away. Even when Lettie gave up of her own accord, around eleven, and limped off to the dining room, he sat on peacefully enough by himself. He was not afraid of dozing off this time—and, in fact, did so. But his night naps were light, and he always enjoyed waking into the deep quiet of nighttime; perhaps this was why he woke so often then. That, and the bathroom, of course.

Reminded, he used Lettie's bathroom once more before he left. He also pulled the umbrella stand over in the way of the door, so that anyone pushing it open incautiously from the porch would meet an obstruction. It was the best he could do to replace her doorchain while he was gone. But he would not leave her long.

He judged the hour to be somewhere soon after midnight. DeKuyper Street lay quiet around him. It was a street of people who worked hard and began early, and only an occasional fast car or some passing gaggle of immature males ever broke its night silence.

The silence within his house had a different quality. He was struck by this, as he mounted its stairs with quiet assurance, until he was able to define the difference. Emptiness, of course (except for the dining room), but an *enclosed* emptiness. Every window and door was shut up tight; trust Dorothea for that.

She had even locked the attic. Against what? Sighing for his poor Martyr, he turned the key and opened the door, and started up the steep enclosed stairwell that led to the attic floor.

Chapter Four

Before Mr. Nicholas had crossed ten feet of floor, he was aware of the other person there with him.

He kept going.

The other person did not move. Still on the narrow ledge of floor behind the stairs—above the door, immobile and almost imperceptibly breathing, someone watched him go.

Presumably watched, if any light was coming in through the windows. Mr. Nicholas, reaching the destination he had set himself, stopped and made random exploration with his stick. No trunks were there. The subject dropped at once from his mind, leaving him without purpose: in this way, he found that he felt some fear.

Realizing this, he at once forced himself round till he faced the stairs, and demanded: "What are you doing there?"

There was no reply. He added: "I see you there—what do you want?"

A small, quick movement, instantly checked, told him

A Friend of Mary Rose

his trap had worked. The person knew him, and knew that he could not see—had almost said so.

"Very well," Mr. Nicholas said then. He folded his hands over his stick and leaned on it. "I will wait. The silence will tell me enough. I know how to listen."

It was a calculated bluff, based on the curious ambivalence of the uninformed to blindness. He was considered either entirely helpless or—when he could prove that he was not—possessed of some mysterious new power, kin to extrasensory perception. The truth lay well to the north of both ideas, of course, but few cared to find that out. So Mr. Nicholas tried his bluff. Besides, he did not know what else to do.

The other's breathing had changed. Unfortunately, so had his own; and when the first whisper began, he could not understand it.

"What?" he said. "What is it?"

The whisper sharpened, until it almost had voice.

"Shut the door! *Shut the door!*"

"Certainly not," Mr. Nicholas said at once. "Why should I? Who are you?"

He suspected it was a boy—not a reassuring suspicion to anyone who listened to the boys along DeKuyper Street nowadays. Except that this one seemed timid.

Mr. Nicholas pressed his advantage—or what he hoped was one.

"I mean you no harm," he said gravely, "but you can't stay here. Now jump down, and get out. Hurry up!"

He heard, after a moment, a light scuffle of sound and then a soft jump—as of sneakered feet. A pause, and then the door was quietly closed. But the person was still there with him! His heart gave a slight irregular movement, and he said indignantly: "Why, what are you—"

"*Shut up!*"

The command was so savage that he obeyed.

Another light scramble followed—a return to that perch, over the door. Perplexed, Mr. Nicholas began: "I want to know—"

"You keep quiet, mister," said the small, savage voice. "Just keep quiet!"

Mr. Nicholas took two steps forward, and stopped.

"Why, you're a girl," he said. "You're a girl! What girl are you?"

"Shut *up!*"

Whatever girl she was, whatever her purpose here, she was close to hysteria. Mr. Nicholas, trying to adjust, did keep quiet a moment.

In that moment, he heard another tread below them in his house. Someone else was there, and coming up from the first floor.

It was the nature of the ascent, more than the fact of it, which kept Mr. Nicholas immobile. It was so curiously undecided. Not only in pauses, although there were several of these, but in the alternate openness and furtiveness of approach. Someone couldn't decide—idiotically, since the time for choice was past—whether he wanted to be heard coming up or not. There was no doubt it was a man. The tread was heavy, even when—after one of those pauses—it tried not to be. Then, at the head of the stairs, the man abandoned concealment. Slowly, openly, he came to the attic door and stopped.

"Hey, kid . . ."

It was a thick voice, slurred and slow. The girl did not reply. Mr. Nicholas could not even hear her breathing.

"Kid—you all right?"

Time went by. He was a slow thinker, this man. Mr. Nicholas did not interfere, but he took a different grasp of his stick.

There was a metallic rasp of sound. The key, turning in the lock.

"Kid—hear that? It's open."

"Come on," he said presently. "It's open. You better go home now."

After a long wait, he became restless, began to mutter.

"Come on, go on home, it's open . . . I'm going," he said, and began to walk with a terrible false loudness—as if he were standing still and trampling in one place.

But he really did move away, and really went clumping down the stairs again.

For the first time since he had taken his stance, Mr. Nicholas allowed his attention to relax. To the girl on the ledge—the presumed girl on the ledge—he said in astonishment: "Who was that?"

"*Shut up!*"

She hadn't relaxed. If anything, she sounded even more feral.

Mr. Nicholas allowed a few seconds to pass, and then said in a low, firm voice: "He can't possibly hear us, he is on the first floor. Now who is that man? Did he lock you in here?"

She replied only by one long, shuddering breath. And a return to ragged breathing. Mr. Nicholas began to understand the depth of her fear, as well as its intensity. She was still scarcely understanding him.

He began to feel very tired.

"Child, what's happened to you? Are you hurt?"

He moved toward her as he spoke—and was checked by another frantic burst of whispering.

"Don't—don't make so much *noise!"*

He stopped moving, but said doggedly, "He can't possibly hear us now, I give you my word. Don't be afraid.

"Do you want me to take you home? Come out, child—I'll take you home."

As he spoke, it occurred to him that whatever the man's intention, by turning that key he had probably locked them in again. But he shelved the thought. The main thing at the moment was to get her calmed down, responding.

She did respond, then. But almost inaudibly.

"He's not gone. He's out there."

Mr. Nicholas, remembering that stagy retreat, was inclined to agree.

"Perhaps," he said, "but it doesn't matter. I'm with you now—when he realizes that, he'll take to his heels fast enough."

"He knows. He doesn't care."

A Friend of Mary Rose

"Nonsense, he has no idea—he'll have the shock of his life. Come along, now—come out of there."

"No, he knows, he doesn't care. He saw you come in."

She was obsessed, unmoving. Unreachable. Except by the thread of this dismal argument, which Mr. Nicholas patiently pursued.

"There was no one in the house or in the grounds when I came in. Believe me—I would know. Just as I knew you were here. Wherever he was, he wasn't around here."

She said unexpectedly, "I know where he went—he went back to get another flashlight. I busted his."

Surely she was a very young girl? Mr. Nicholas felt sure of it, with this first sound of a recognizable voice from her. His tone changed, with the opinion, and became at once gentler and more authoritative.

"Would you rather I went down first and chased him away? Then you won't be afraid to come out, will you?"

"*No*—don't go! Don't—"

"All right," he said. "All right, I won't do anything you don't agree to. But don't be afraid."

She was suddenly explosive with rage.

"*I'm not afraid*—quit saying that! I'm not afraid! But I've got some sense and you haven't—you stupid old man, you old dumb, stupid old blind man, you—don't know anything—"

"I know you're making a lot of noise," he said.

She wasn't, even then. But the charge made her suck in silence, sharply, and hold it. She was also, he thought, struggling not to cry.

Presently Mr. Nicholas went on: "Don't you understand that this man believes you are here alone? As soon as he realizes that you are not, you will have nothing more to fear from him. And I hope you are not—I hope you know that you can trust me. Do you know who I am?"

She said, after a long silence, "I wasn't after your money."

"Well," he said, "you would be welcome to any you found. Do you know my name?"

She took time to reply to this, too. And said finally: "I didn't mean what I said, before."

"It's of no consequence. But you must not—you must allow me to help you, child."

"You don't have to help me. I know what I'm going to do."

"What?" he said, patient.

There was a long pause. Then she said: "See this?"

"No. What is it?"

To his surprise, she was confused by her mistake.

"Oh. Well, it's—it's a brick. From the chimley. The minute he comes in that door, I can get him from up here. That's why you've got to be quiet, mister! Because he'll know if he hears anything—and he'll see you, too, if you stand right there! He's got a flashlight now, and he'll see you the minute he opens the door! Please mister—please come back here!"

All at once, for whatever reason, she had accepted him as an ally. It was certainly not the alliance he wanted, to be asked to help with her childish, murderous plan, but it was a beginning. If he was ever to get her unfrozen, off that ledge, it could only be by talking.

He went on talking.

"I don't believe he will come back, you know. He didn't like having to come back and unlock the door, did he?"

"No, he's scared." There was a ghost of satisfaction in her voice. It faded, as she went on: "He'll come back, though—he's got to. See, he's got to find out if I'm all right, or what. That's why we got to be quiet, so he'll think I'm *not*. Then I can get him."

An abyss opened somewhere inside Mr. Nicholas. Not in the head; lower.

"*Are* you all right?" he managed to say.

"Yes, only please come back here—please! You don't have to come all the way, just so he won't see you—please!"

His mind still groped under shock. What did she mean, the man had to come back and find out if she was "all right, or what"? Why should she not be all right? What had happened to her—*how had she been left?*

He was suddenly convinced that she did not come out to him because she could not. Then he remembered the way she had scrambled down to close the door, and up again, and in a confusion of relief he started toward her.

"*Look out for the steps!*"

"All right," he said, shaken by her panic. "All right, child, I know. . . ."

He found the stairwell and began skirting it with his

stick, like a small offer of reassurance to her. She was entirely attentive; and when he came to where the roof sloped, near her perch, she began to make small movements. They were naturally made, not convulsive any more: she was coming to meet him, or crawling into some better position. Her breathing was better, too. And all her attention was on him—she did not hear the small thud of sound in the house below.

Mr. Nicholas heard it. It was far below, perhaps in the front hall. He could not decide what had caused it.

She whispered suddenly, "What is it?" and all her movements ceased.

He replied calmly, stretching out his hand:

"Can you reach me, child?"

Her only answer was a convulsive scramble—backward again, away from him.

He said, "Now don't be foolish, give me your—"

"Wait. *Wait.*"

He had lost her to her terrors once more.

Helpless, he listened with her, and the next sound was audible to them both. It was, in fact, the crack of the third step from the bottom, and it was followed by so long a pause that Mr. Nicholas felt both repulsion and surprise.

What was he standing there so long for?

Mr. Nicholas began seriously to consider the attic door. If it was really locked—and it probably was—then there was no use frightening the fellow off before he unlocked it. And the girl seemed to be right: this was a badly frightened man. The question was whether or not he would come even as far as the attic door again. Every sound he made seemed to throw him into a paralysis of caution.

Then there came a strike against the wall below, as if from some loss of balance. That was nearer. He was coming on.

But coming on in a way that Mr. Nicholas did not understand, or like at all. It really seemed more animal than human to be drawn—and redrawn—to an object in such a manner! With so much fear and indecision, and yet with such helpless purpose. Surely his fear was not of the child, and if he knew or suspected that she was no longer alone, why was he coming back at all?

With growing sobriety, Mr. Nicholas changed the position of his body and of his stick. He knew there were men—conditions of man—beyond concern with discovery or shame. Obsessed creatures, who could be checked only by force. He began to think it possible that such a creature was coming up to them now.

And that the man's fear was not of them, but of what he had done. Or what he meant to do.

This time the pause seemed interminable. Mr. Nicholas was careful not to break it. In that long listening, he was coming into agreement with the girl's insistence on surprise. Because they had not much else between them, God knew, to substitute for force.

He still meant to call out, but not until the man tried to enter. At the same time, he now planned to strike down hard with his stick. It was a blackthorn, and heavy—if it should chance to connect it would give a solid blow. But he was not—like the poor child with her brick—counting on any knockout. No; surprise must be their weapon, as total and violent as possible; and their success, he hoped, another retreat on the man's part. At least a long enough one so that Mr. Nicholas might go quickly down and get the key on their side of the door, and lock them in.

For he was convinced by now that no time-weakened old man would get this child safe-conduct through an empty house, an empty yard, with such an animal stalking her. Force alone would do it—and even combined, their only real force lay in a chance of first surprise. Beyond that, Mr. Nicholas really feared that he would not be able to defend her.

Without relaxing, he waited out the long seconds between sounds. Beside him, the girl was shaking hard. He could almost feel the tremor of sound her flesh made against the attic boards. Could almost imagine that other listener hearing it, too, who wanted so badly to hear something!

But they gave him nothing. They were able to do that.

And in the end he went away. With new decision—in what supposed privacy of intention Mr. Nicholas could not imagine—the man turned and tiptoed to the downstairs hall, and out of hearing.

He had not touched the door, or even come near it.

Chapter Five

Mr. Nicholas was amazed at the girl's resilience.

Although she gave no sign until he spoke to her—and none for several moments after that—her first whispering turned into such a torrent that he gave up trying to reply. Not a torrent of terror, either—she was rocketed up, almost to euphoria! And rather inclined to boast.

She had been all ready, with her brick—they would really have given it to him—see, she said he was scared, didn't she? Wasn't she right? He knew she'd be laying for him—but he didn't know where! He didn't even know there was a place over the door! And boy, if he ever came back, if he ever came in—

"Oh, hush, child," Mr. Nicholas murmured.

His own imperative was to sit down, and he was having difficulties. There was no place to sit but the floor, and rather severe leg tremors—due to fatigue—made it hard to let himself down so far without falling. What he needed was to find the wall and let himself down between that and his stick, but the wall here sloped sharply, and in an unaccustomed confusion, he forgot.

"*Oh!*" she said, crying out for his bump. Then came scrambles, and clutching, that nearly took his remaining balance away. He wasted no breath in protest until he was down, in spite of her help, with his back against the wall and his temporarily useless legs laid out in front of him.

Then he said sharply: "Now control yourself, girl—control yourself! Be still!"

To soften this, he grumbled on: "What a hair-trigger girl you are—I'm surprised you didn't start whacking the door with that brick of yours. I'm surprised you didn't whack me!"

"Oh, no," she said at once. "I knew it was you. I mean, first I just knew it wasn't him, but then I could hear your stick, and I knew it was you."

She meant when he first arrived, of course. When he had sorted this out, he did feel some surprise. It had not occurred to him that he might have been her target.

"Well," he said, "thank you for using your head, then. Instead of mine."

Now she had begun to hiccup, a disarming sound. Her hands he remembered as small and thin, but with strength. He was sorry he had pushed them off so fussily and lost his chance to discover what she was. She sat carefully separate from him now. But this close, she smelled more child than girl.

There was also an odor of blood, which he found himself hesitant to ask about—and then, considering it, to speak of at all.

She was still very keyed up. After a brief struggle with her hiccups she lost patience, and began whispering to him again between clucks.

"Gee, I didn't know what to do about you, mister, I didn't want to get you into trouble, too, but I didn't know what to do! And then I thought maybe if you just got your money and went away you'd be all right, because he didn't have anything against you—and then I thought that would be even better, because then he'd think you left the door unlocked and I already got out, and he wouldn't know where to look for me, so he wouldn't bother. I wish we had done like that," she said wistfully.

"But it never occurred to you to ask me for help?"

He had not meant this as a reproach, but perhaps it came out that way. She answered it quickly, as if it were.

"Oh, sure, I would have, only—well, I didn't know if you might report me, that was all."

"Dear God, child—report you?"

"Well, I didn't know about you then, just how you were supposed to be kind of . . ." She couldn't think of a word for what he was supposed to be. Or not a polite one.

"Mean? Crabby?"

"No," she said, and found it: "Strick." Then old anxiety woke in her. "I wasn't after your money, mister—I swear to God I wasn't! If it was laying right in the middle of the floor, I wouldn't have touched it. I wouldn't!"

He said wearily, "I believe you. But why did you come—did that man bring you here?"

"Bring me! No! I just wanted to see inside, that's all—just see what it was like, if it was so fancy, and everything. And they said she left a lot of stuff—but I wasn't going to take anything!"

"Was he here when you came, then?"

"No, I don't think so. Maybe he was," she said, considering. "I guess he could have been, all right. See, it was him told me about the window—like a joke, you know? He said somebody told him it was broke, in case he wanted to get in and have a look for the old—for your money, mister. Like a joke? He said it probably wasn't true though. But it was, I looked on the way home, and it was broke all right. Not the glass, so you could see—just the thing in the middle that would lock it, if it wasn't broke. You wouldn't notice unless you looked."

"There were no broken locks on my windows," said Mr. Nicholas. "Who is this man?"

His question made her silent—or perhaps her own story did, evoking again that trap she had fallen into.

When she whispered to him again, it was a dispirited sound.

"We ought to be listening. He might come back. . . ."

"I am listening. All the time."

It was true. He had not for one moment tried to foretell what such a man might or might not do. All he had known, in their first moments of respite, was that he needed time to get his legs back; and this he had allowed himself to hope for. Apparently he was to have it. Sitting, he flexed these now, and found them fairly responsive.

"Do you think he will, mister?"

Her bravado was gone. She wanted him to say, No. He considered what it was he did have to say to her, and decided to begin with the locked door.

"Child," he said, and then, impatient: "What is your name?"

"My name?"

"Yes, to call you by. What are you called?"

"Oh," she said. "Well, it's—Mary Rose."

She was selecting this name for him. He sighed, and accepted it.

"Well, Mary Rose, I've been thinking about this business of taking you down through the house—"

"No," she said. "No, mister!"

"Just a minute. We can't do that, you see. I'm afraid that when your friend turned the key—"

"He's not my friend!"

"I beg your pardon," he said, vexed with himself. "I'm sorry, Mary Rose. That's just a way of speaking."

"It's all right. I guess I did used to speak to him," she admitted. "Gee—how would you know an old man could be so crazy? I just thought he was kind of stupid. All the kids did."

He said, "An old man?"

"No, I didn't mean that, mister. Just like—grown up."

Between her anxiety not to offend him and her curious sense of secrecy, he was finding it very hard to talk to her. But it was necessary to keep trying.

"Yes. Well, about the door—you see, I had left it unlocked, and so when—the key was turned again, that would naturally have locked it."

"I know. But it's all right, he'll think he did it. He's *stupid*."

"Yes. Well, the point is, Mary Rose, that since we are locked in, and since we would much rather be out, the only thing to do is to break the window and—and call."

"Break the window!"

"Certainly. It's my window."

"But he'll hear us! You couldn't do that without him hearing us! He's the only one that *will* hear us," she said wildly, "and then he'll know we're laying for him, and we won't have a chance, mister! Don't do it—please don't do it—"

"Mary Rose, be quiet."

Instantly, she was.

"There is no one coming," he said, taken aback. "You don't have to be that quiet. Just let me discuss this with you, will you?"

She still made no sound. And then he heard a small, ragged sigh.

"My hiccups are gone. . . ."

"Well, I'm glad. But will you let me finish what I'm trying to say? Then I'll listen to you. There is no other way to have a sensible discussion."

"Yes. Sure. Only—I don't think that's such a good idea, mister."

"Well, let's examine it. Your main objection is that you think no one will hear us except this man. That's extremely improbable. If we act together, and promptly—if we both begin to shout as loudly as we can the moment I have knocked the glass from the window—and I can do that very quickly—it is simply not possible that no one will hear us. Don't you realize how many people occupy the houses across the street? And the boardinghouse next door?"

He waited, to make her answer.

"Yes . . . I guess so. But they might not . . ."

"Might not *what*?"

"They might not come. . . . They might not know who we are."

"But what possible difference can that make? When you hear someone shouting, 'Help, police!' in the middle of the night, you don't care who it is! You report it, as fast as you can, of course. I assure you, Mary Rose, this is our only sensible course, and we really must not waste any more time. Now help me up, like a good girl, and—"

"Mister! Wait!"

Although he had scarcely moved, she was clutching him with all her wiry strength. But how small she was! Surely not even twelve—?

In this new dismay, he missed what she was saying.

"What? What is it?"

"The *cops*, mister! What would we say? What would they do to us? If we yell like you said, somebody's going to call the cops!"

He said helplessly, "Mary Rose, I don't understand you. At a time like this, you're afraid of the police?"

But before he got the question out, he understood that

Elizabeth Fenwick

it was useless. For whatever reason, she was. He would have to start all over on this premise.

"All right," he said. "Now listen to me. This is my house. No one—*no one*—can object to your being here if I do not. Do you understand that? And I do not object. You have my full and complete permission to be here."

"They won't believe you," she said sadly.

"They will. They have no choice. I'm the only one who can make a complaint, and I won't make it. Now if you are afraid of what your parents—"

"But why would we say we were here? They'll think we were doing something bad," she said earnestly. "They'll think we were up here doing something bad!"

It was like crossing a swamp. Trying to run.

He drew a long breath, and abandoned the sticky ground of reason. For whatever fantastic treetop this child lived in.

"All right, supposing that's true—which it most certainly is not. Then I would be taking an equal chance with you. And I agree to take it—rather than wait here all night at the mercy of a criminal lunatic!"

The minute the words were out, he regretted them: the ugly adult words bursting out like a new horror for her, that she would not have found for herself.

But she seemed scarcely to have heard. Lost in her own maze, she murmured on: "And how would we explain about the door being locked? If you—"

"Mary Rose, we haven't time for all this. You will have to take my word for it that you will *not* get into trouble—

by allowing yourself to be rescued—from the very real danger you are in *now*."

He made this as clear as he could, speaking slowly. When she said nothing, he added: "And I promise I will do all I can to help you. Now, and later. Do you believe me?"

"Yes . . ."

"Then get up, and give me your hand."

"But you don't have to help me. . . . I know what I'm going to do, I got this brick. . . ."

In exhaustion, she had gone back to her first premise—and with a limpness that alarmed him. His attempts to reason had only ended by putting her into a stupor: of indecision, of fatigue. They had come to the end of the usefulness of words.

Turning his stick, he deliberately struck the hard end hard against the floor. Only once; but the report was explosive. And to the cry this wrung from her he added harshly: "Be quiet!

"Now get up," he said. "And give me your hand."

Softly, hopelessly, she began to cry.

"Hurry!"

Still crying, in clumsy small movements she started to obey. He did not let himself move or speak lest this distract her. Weeping, she crawled over him, stumbled up onto her sneakered feet. He put up his hand, groping till he found hers. She let it be taken.

"Move back, Mary Rose," he said. "Pull."

Between the lever of her grasp (or his grasp of her)

and the wall behind him, he got back on his legs. Then, gently pushing her before him, he came forward from under the roof and stood erect.

His legs held.

She leaned against him, and he put his free arm awkwardly about her. Her head came only to his chest—the hair was rough, and short like a boy's. Her little shoulder felt like a wrist.

"Don't cry any more," he said gently. "Remember what we are going to do. You will have to shout very loudly—can you do that? Do you want to take my stick and break the window?"

She shook her head—rolling it back and forth upon his chest.

"Well, come along then. Watch me break it."

She did not move. She was guarding her crying, aware of it—perhaps enjoying her refuge, and unwilling to give it up. But he knew that it was no real refuge. And there was not time to pretend.

"Come along, child."

He began to move, moving her with him. She came leaning, in a childish dawdle, which he bore.

Then she stiffened and stood still.

There had been a faint sharpish sound the moment before, but not in the house. Something, somewhere out on the street, had broken or fallen—he did not yet place the sound, and was bewildered by its effect on her.

"What is it?" he said. "What's the matter?"

"The streetlight—he's knocked out the streetlight—"

"What? What do you mean?"

"With a rock—he busted the streetlight!"

He could scarcely hear her. Her body was rigid with terror. The strangeness of this new attack, if it was one, left him at a loss.

"But what difference does that make? It doesn't matter if people can't see us up here," he said, groping, "they can certainly still hear us! Come on—"

"But I can't see! Oh, he's coming back—he's coming back—and *I can't see!*"

It was dark in the attic now. That was it.

Reassured, he said at once: "But I can! The dark makes no difference to me, you know that! Now let go of me, child—here, take my hand. Give me your hand!"

But he could not rearrange her—she was gripping his coat, his body, in such frozen fear that they were both immobilized. Worse, a frenzy of whispers was pouring from her—cutting her off from his voice like a loss of hearing.

". . . my brick, I got to get back there and get my brick, I got to get back there before he comes—oh, it's so dark—I can't see, I can't see—"

"Stop it, stop it—*be quiet!*" he commanded. But the words had lost their magic for her, were not even heard. And when in desperation he began to shake her, she only twisted herself free and darted off—became lost to him entirely.

He could hear her blundering about, sobbing and whispering to herself, and fear seized him, too: that she would hurt herself, that she would fall into the stairwell in one of those blind rushes. Pushing his stick before him, still urgently saying her name, he started after her—a hopeless chase, but impossible to abandon. Then she, perhaps blindly answering his voice, ran back toward him, and they met violently.

"I can't find the place, I can't find the place! Oh, mister, take me back, I got to get my brick—"

He muttered, breathless from their hard meeting, "Take hold of my coat. Here! Give me your hand, take hold of my coat!"

This time she obeyed—or at least let her grip be altered so that he could, however awkwardly, move again and draw her behind him. He lost no time in doing so.

Unfortunately, at the moment he did not know exactly where they were. They had done so much gyrating during their separation he had lost his bearings. If she had been a little calmer, he would have made her look to find the windows before they started: as he remembered, these were always to some degree visible. But as things were, he judged it simpler just to set off, pushing his stick before him and holding his other hand half raised to meet any descent of the sloping roof. As soon as he reached any part of the wall or roof, he had only to determine which part it was and then the entire map of the attic would fall into place within his mind. And very soon he felt his hand touch and then follow a descending rafter.

He changed direction, rapidly passing along the slope to determine its length. For a brief, passionate moment he regretted that Dorothea had not in fact betrayed him, and left some familiar object to tell him where it, and he, stood. But nothing was left.

He was continuing intently to finger his way when the girl behind him burst out whispering again.

"Oh, *no*—oh, that's the *window!*"

"Where?" he said sharply. "Ahead? *Which window?*"

Like some echo of his words, he heard quite clearly the report of the sprung board by the bathroom door. Someone had stepped on it.

He said nothing—it was not necessary; the girl had heard, too.

They fell into double silence, intense and brief. In that silence, she let go of his coat.

He still did not speak—not even her name. He only reached across his braced stick to recapture her—but she was gone. That sound had told her where to go, where the stair would be, and she was gone to reach it in total new obedience. She would not obey him now, and he could not match the rapid stealth with which she was leaving him: almost running across the floor on her sneaker-clad feet. He listened dully to hear her fall into the stairwell, but she did not. In some desperate, almost noiseless scramble, she was regaining her lost perch.

And he had, automatically still trying, found his bearings: he was standing near the window, the back window. Overlooking a double row of deserted back yards.

Into their silence, the man turned the knob of the attic door.

Chapter Six

The holding door gave him no trouble. This time, he meant to come in. The key was turned again, and the door opened, and in that moment Mr. Nicholas regained the power to move.

At the same time, the girl fell. Fell, or was pulled down—he could not tell. But there was no mistaking the cascade of thumps that marked her fall into the stairwell, or the rage of growling with which the man received her.

Pushing his stick before him, Mr. Nicholas began to run across the floor.

When the girl screamed, he stopped dead. She screamed twice, sounds of animal pain, which Mr. Nicholas answered with all the force of his voice.

"Let her alone!" he shouted. "For God's sake, let the child alone!"

He might have been an echo, a ghost of that attic, for all the difference he made. Some scuffle, hard and violent, continued until his stick reached the edge of the floor. Then it stopped.

There was not a sound of the girl. Only of the panting, lurching man down below. Then only the panting.

Mr. Nicholas struck the floor as hard as he could, and then raised his stick high.

"You murderer!" he called. "I know you! Get out of here—get out of this house!"

The faintest grayness bloomed upon his vision. Some radiance was turned full on him: the flashlight. Mr. Nicholas stared sternly, desperately downward, beneath his raised stick.

"Get out of here!" he said loudly. "Get out!"

Like a slow reply, the man whispered: "Why, you dirty old bastard, you. You dirty old bastard . . ."

It was not even a voice. To Mr. Nicholas, listening as a stifling man might breathe—with his whole concentration in the effort—no clue of humanity came with the words. Barely the words themselves, on harsh, heavy breath.

Mr. Nicholas said nothing, and stepped back. To this invitation, the man slowly began to ascend, still whispering.

". . . you doing up here with the kid, eh? Dirty old bastard . . . dirty old . . ."

With a sudden, sideways slash, Mr. Nicholas brought his stick down. It was caught, and held. After one tug, Mr. Nicholas let it remain briefly in this double hold. Then, with all his force, he thrust forward.

The man's backward stagger nearly pulled him down into the well, too. There was a moment when the stick was nearly free . . . and then he knew his legs would

63

not do it, would not give him the support he needed, and at once Mr. Nicholas let go. Doubly freed, the stick clattered down the steps and stopped.

The man laughed.

At first, Mr. Nicholas did not recognize the flat, open-mouthed sound for what it was. Then he identified and dismissed it, continuing slowly to back away—a magnet, if nothing more. And a magnet that could grip and hold, when the time came.

Going slowly backward across his attic, Mr. Nicholas began to feel that the time would never come. He had, in his last resource, invented a game too satisfactory to this dead-minded beast he drew after him—at once a respite and a long chance to threaten, which the man was in no haste to alter. With his flashlight steadily trained—but not too near, there was no warmth in the grayness—he came shuffling after, spewing slow obscenities for his pleasure as he came.

There was no doubt that they pleased him, that his slow mind took pleasure in groping out words for the girl's debauching, and grotesquely attaching them to the old man in his view. Mr. Nicholas, far past squeamishness or any sense of shock, listened with great care to the voice. But it never became one. It was not that the man took any counter-care to deceive. He had no need to. He was producing sounds at the level of one in delirium, or in sleep, and no more recognizably. Because no thought was there, no individual voice ever appeared.

Mr. Nicholas was also trying to gauge to what degree the man was drunk. There was no doubt that he had been drinking; the still air stank of him by now. He muttered and moved like someone far gone. Yet he had caught Mr. Nicholas's stick soon enough. No doubt he had caught the girl's arm on its descent, too, in order to pull her down so quickly. And he had succeeded in breaking the streetlight with a stone, no matter after how many tries. Mr. Nicholas decided there was no use trying to guess how much of the man's behavior was due to drink and how much due to sheer animalism released by the drinking. The main thing was that he was still physically competent.

Resigning himself to this, Mr. Nicholas took the initiative and stood still. The man was not prepared for this. As at the thrust stick, he lost balance. The light's grayness went away, came back. The drone of loose words stopped.

A younger man might have leaped forward then, with some chance of success. Mr. Nicholas did not even try. He simply stood, keeping his hands open and ready—thank God, they were still strong.

The other did not like this stopping. For himself, he chose to keep in motion, in a slow, peripheral circling of the motionless man. He made no more sound except for his shuffling and breathing; perhaps he was engaged in some attempt at thought. Mr. Nicholas waited, turning as necessary to keep their encounter face to face.

Mercifully soon, the man struck. It must have been with the flashlight, to cause such a painful blow. Fortunately he caught Mr. Nicholas's shoulder instead of the portion of the head he had no doubt aimed for—and in addition, he dropped the flashlight. But these mishaps only ended his attempt at planned attack, and he reverted much more successfully to a simple seizure of Mr. Nicholas, which immediately brought them both to the floor.

Then Mr. Nicholas took hold. He took the best and most secure hold he could manage, with each hand, and locked on—in one case to the underarm part of a jacket, and in the other to a fistful of hair, of which there seemed to be plenty. Still conscious, still not too much distracted by pain, Mr. Nicholas felt that these gripping hands of his were well placed, and would not now fail no matter what happened. Even in unconsciousness, even—if that was to be—in death, his hands would not unlock, this beast would not get free of him to go back to the girl at the foot of the stairs. And if he tried, he would have to drag Mr. Nicholas's body along with him. The hands would not unlock.

At first the man was distracted by the grip on his hair, and tried to prize it off. While he was fumbling, Mr. Nicholas heard the child trying to come silently up the stairs. If anything could have loosened his grip, the weakening despair that flooded him then would have done it. For she was after—oh, God, she was after that brick again. . . .

The fumbling stopped, and two savage hands seized his throat. No cry from Mr. Nicholas could have passed them. But with all his heart, his mind—his bursting mind—he thought to her: *Run, run, run away.* . . .

He heard her suddenly clatter down the stairs.

A Friend of Mary Rose

The hands heard her. They did not slacken, but were still. Then they were gone.

Mr. Nicholas's hands did not unlock.

His heavy old body hung from them—twisted, jerked, flung, struck, kicked, his body still depended from those hands that were his mind now, his life, all that remained of him. And the hands held. As long as he knew of them at all, he knew they held.

When it was always dark, sound was the light you woke to. The mind's real darkness then became no sound; and this was surprisingly rare. There was always some sort of sound, somewhere, to a total listener; and so when Mr. Nicholas began to be aware of himself—as a consciousness, and yet as a consciousness within a void—he seriously considered whether he had not entered some form of afterlife.

As much as by the void, in which he knew he lay, he was influenced by the altered quality of his own consciousness. He was himself, and yet not his known self; and this more than anything convinced him.

To his faint surprise, he found that he did not know what to do. His first impulse, one of respect, was to offer prayer. And yet, what prayer? His altered consciousness, feebly revolving all the known words, could find none which seemed appropriate to say *now*. And then he came, as an afterthought, to the Gloria Patri—so brief that it was almost gone before he recognized it: . . . As it was in the beginning, is now, and ever shall be, world without end . . .

Was it even a prayer? Yet his anxiety was subsiding, surely this was the one. Firmly, he thought his prayer again and then—closing his mind—submitted himself once more to the new void.

After a while there were hands, a child's hands.

He murmured without stirring (and somehow without sound): "Get in, get in, don't catch cold"; but the child was crying.

He made himself wake further. Some very pleasant sense of dreaming still clung to him, and he could not at once tell which child this was. But he put his hand up to it. There was pain somewhere, too.

The crying child had begun to whisper, "Get up, get up—oh, mister, don't be dead, don't die—get up—"

Mary Rose.

He said her name, but she paid no attention and only went on whispering, ". . . get up, please get up, I'll help you—I got your stick, here's your stick—please get up, mister, I'll help you. . . ."

"No," he said, breaking into this firmly but kindly. "No, I can't do that."

There was silence for a time. He could go back to sleep.

Then she spoke to him. In a real voice, neither a whisper nor a mutter. It was the first he had heard of her voice, and the surprise of it woke him entirely.

"Are you sure? Did you try?"

It was his own normal voice that had evoked hers, of course, and so he used it again.

A Friend of Mary Rose

"No, I haven't tried, Mary Rose."

"Aren't you going to?"

How desolate she sounded! He turned his head, and became aware of the floor boards beneath it, and the capacity for pain within it. And of much else.

"Child, what are you doing back here?" he said, appalled. "Where is that man?"

"It's all right," she assured him quickly. "Don't worry, it's all right! I locked everything, with the chains up—even the door down to the cellar! And I put those shutters over the busted window, with that fasten they got, and I pushed that big chest over in front—he couldn't get back in here in a million years!"

Something had gone very wrong. He could not yet grasp what it was.

"But why did you do that?" he asked; and said, believing it, "I told you to run home!"

"I know, I did—I did, mister! First I was going to try and get him off you, and then I didn't know if I could—he twisted my arm pretty bad, and I couldn't work it. It's not broke," she said quickly, "it's just twisted. But anyway I thought if I made a noise like running away he'd get off you and come after me. I can run about sixty times faster than him any day. And I was going to tell Bud about you, honest I was—I would have told him, and he would have come back here and got you. But he wasn't home. His car wasn't in the yard, I guess he stayed at Lou's. Sometimes he does that."

Out of his total confusion, Mr. Nicholas asked: "Who is Bud?"

Elizabeth Fenwick

"My brother."

She was crouched close against him, speaking very fast, with long pauses. Recurrent small spasms of shuddering went through her, and echoed in Mr. Nicholas, but she paid no attention to them. Except for these, her breathing was fairly regular, and her voice—her small, high voice—seemed normal too.

"You're bleeding," he said.

"It's just my nose, it bleeds all the time. If I fight, or if anybody hits me on the head. Everybody around here knows not to hit me on the head. Except him." She burst out: "He's in our yard—in that old Chevy that don't run. I don't know if he passed out or what. Or if he's just *waiting* there!"

Mr. Nicholas sighed in defeat.

"I don't understand this, Mary Rose. You were home? You went home, and then came back here?"

"Well," she said, "sure—I had to go *somewheres* fast!"

But he had infected her with doubt. She began to argue.

"See, our back door don't lock. And I could see him out there in the Chevy, I could see him. And he could see Bud's car wasn't there, he'd know he wasn't home just the same as I would. And everybody knows it's pretty hard to wake up my dad, and he isn't—he's pretty old anyway. So I thought, what if he comes in here and does the same thing to my dad? Like he did to you, mister. So I sneaked out the front way and came back here—this place locks up good. If he came in our place and I wasn't there, he wouldn't stay.

A Friend of Mary Rose

"I put up all those chains," she went on presently. "Boy, she has them everywhere, doesn't she? But it's a good thing for us, though."

She meant his daughter-in-law. Confusion began to overtake Mr. Nicholas.

"She's a fearful woman," he murmured. "Always was. Yet nothing has ever happened to Dorothea, that I know of. . . ."

"Even if he comes back here and gets into the cellar, he couldn't get up here. I don't think he will, though. He might have passed out, I couldn't tell. And anyway the light's on in Millers' kitchen and that means it's after four o'clock. He won't hang around any more so close to daylight, he won't do that."

The light in Millers' kitchen. What kitchen this was— what kitchen had become Millers' kitchen, he had no idea. And yet he saw that light, that beacon, that promise of release which she had ignored. A little groan escaped him, at the thought of the wakened household, able to defend her, to call in help. Why had she run away from it, back to this ghost house—and to him?

"Oh, Mary Rose—why didn't you go there?" he murmured.

"Go where?"

He had forgotten the name.

She said, "You mean to *Millers'?*"

Apparently he did. It was her turn to be bewildered.

"Gee, I wouldn't go there, mister! I guess you don't know what they think about us—they hate us worse than rats! They're the ones that keep reporting us all the time,

71

Elizabeth Fenwick

they want to get me put in Children's! Only Bud won't let them," she said quickly. "He makes good money, and he might get married, too. Only I hope it's not Lou. . . ."

She fell quiet, pursuing some uneasy speculation. He could not follow her any more. Nor, somehow, could he get back—back out of the maze she had led him into. At its far end shone a light, a kitchen light, that they might not approach. He could not remember what light this was, or even if it was real.

At his chest, his vest button, her fingers worried lightly. His main awareness came to center in this touching, which was like his cat's when it wanted to wake him. This was not his cat, he did not know where his cat was—and yet he recognized a similar persistent message. He ought to get up.

She suggested as much, presently.

"Couldn't you get up, mister? Couldn't you try?"

"I got your stick," she said.

He heard her hunting it, beside them. Then the knob end came to his hand. He closed his fingers round it.

"If you could get up, we could just go home when it gets light. Nobody would have to know. I could help you."

He had, at that moment, no quarrel with any of this. But he did not move.

"Bud might not even come back," she went on, explaining their position to him. "He might go right to work. I could call him and he'd come and get you, except how would I say I knew you were here? He wouldn't

A Friend of Mary Rose

think it was anything bad," she said firmly. "He knows I wouldn't ever do anything like that, because that's the one thing he couldn't stop them taking me, if I got into that kind of trouble. Besides, I wouldn't anyway. He knows that. But he'd know I busted in."

She considered this. Mr. Nicholas, relieved to be still following, waited. He gathered that they were not afraid of Bud, but that he presented some sort of problem.

"I don't mind a licking," she said.

"No," said Mr. Nicholas, to his own surprise.

"But the worse thing is if he doesn't give me a licking, if he just gets fed up. See, like he says, by now I ought to be able to look after myself, and help with Dad, too—and I *do*," she said. "We don't need anybody, he doesn't have to marry Lou! He'd be crazy to marry Lou," she said with sudden passion. "If he doesn't want to already, he'd *hate* it if he did! And believe me, mister, she doesn't act so nice when she doesn't have to. She doesn't want us. I don't care what she says, she doesn't want us. She wants Bud, but she don't want us, and she'd get rid of us pretty quick, too, if they got married!"

Mr. Nicholas's fingers tightened on his stick. He believed her.

"But when—if something like this happens, then sometimes he really gets fed up. Mostly he just gets mad, and yells at Dad, or gives me a licking—that's all right. But I hate it when he gets fed up. I *hate* it. . . .

"Someday he'll get so fed up he'll marry Lou," she said. Her voice was hushed with that fear.

In his own bed, Mr. Nicholas always rose first on one

elbow and then put his legs over the edge of the bed. Once he got into that position, he was as good as up. Or if he were sitting up with a wall behind him—they had managed that, he and Mary Rose. But the problem here, he began to realize, was not the lack of support, or a place to put his legs over, but a curious lassitude that kept him from making any beginning. He lay and *thought* movement, but somehow he made none.

Could he move? Convulsively, he pushed an arm out from his body—and it went. Now if he could roll sideways and brace upon it . . . But at these first efforts, she eagerly seized upon him and began to help. To *try* to help—by tugging him upright.

The result of this was such a vertigo of pain that Mr. Nicholas could not even speak, to protest. He could not get loose from her, he could not make her stop—and he began seriously to fear that the child was going to kill him.

The horror of this idea—that he might suddenly sag lifeless in her poor little arms, in this deserted house—was probably what got him upright at last. Certainly none of the equipment by which he had to raise himself could have done it. Even when he finally stood—or hung—between his stick and Mary Rose's small body, he could hardly believe in their accomplishment.

Or be glad of it. He felt, to tell the truth, like a homemade Lazarus—a clear mistake.

But there was no doubt of the child's joy. She was incoherent with it, and with praise for him.

"See, you could do it, mister—you could do it! I didn't

A Friend of Mary Rose

do it, I *couldn't*—I was so scared! But you did it, mister! Oh, you got up so *good*," she cried, embracing him.

Her embrace hurt him. Her voice hurt him. He could not reflect one particle of her joy. But here he was, raised, sober, with a clearing mind.

He said glumly, "Hush, child. Let go . . ." and began to try if his legs would hold.

Chapter Seven

Somehow they got down the attic stairs.

Although he had no spare energy to remonstrate, the child quickly learned to restrain her rough help. By the time they reached the stairs she was behaving as intelligently as a guide dog after months of training, staying close for support but never tugging or pulling at him. He felt some pride for her, and intended to speak of it when he could.

Thank God, his mind had cleared. And he had become more familiar with the sources of his pain and able to define them. Nothing vital seemed to be broken.

On the other hand, his general condition was extremely poor; and leaning between the wall and his stick—with Mary Rose breathing anxiously beside him—he had to admit that this was as far as he could go, just now.

It was going to be a blow to the child. Her goal was the dining-room chairs, where she seemed to envision them sitting in a civilized manner and waiting for day-

A Friend of Mary Rose

light. It had also occurred to her (she was a very bright child) that if he waited on a chair, they would avoid the problem of getting him off the floor again. She was right; but he simply was not able to go on.

He was going to have to speak of this soon. Already, with controlled but rising anxiety, she had twice asked him if he was all right.

He drew a careful breath and answered:

"Yes. Thank you. But I am going to rest in my room now. Come with me."

Most of this journey could be made against the wall; and in addition, he was remembering the radiator cover. This was built in; Dorothea would hardly have gone to the trouble of removing it. And it could be sat on. He wished he had the energy to explain these things to Mary Rose, who was behaving in a disconsolate—almost a frantic—way, at this change in plan. But he had to keep on, wordless, leaning his way down the wall, until at last he opened the familiar door and crept in.

She followed, still trying to urge him back.

". . . like a piggyback, see? I can do it, honest I can, I'm strong and I'd be careful! And you could keep one hand on the rail if you wanted, but you wouldn't have to. I'd be like your stick, see, only better, and you could lean right over on me, so you wouldn't hardly be walking down on your own legs at all! Please try it, mister— please!"

Around the wall, halfway along the next. And there it was. He found his radiator cover and began to lower himself on it. And was seated at last. He put both hands over his stick and found a balance. Now there was no part of him without support. The relief was enormous.

Silenced at last, the girl had come to stand in front of him. Suddenly she gave a small cry. It jarred him, but he didn't move.

"Mister! I can see light around you! It's getting light, look!" She added hastily, "I mean, the window's all gray, like—you can see it. I can see the whole shape of you!"

"Good," he murmured, not stirring.

Then she laughed. A real laugh, of pure delight.

"Hey, it's tomorrow! Get it? Like all that stuff was yesterday, and it's not yesterday any more—it's tomorrow!"

She was absolutely enchanted by her discovery. He wouldn't have interfered with her logic for the world. Now everything began to interest and please her.

"Hey, that's a pretty good seat," she said, exploring it. "What is it? What's in it? She sure left a lot of good things, didn't she?"

He muttered, "Don't knock my stick . . ." and she replied, content, "No, it's okay, I can see that, too. I can see *every*thing, sort of! Honest I can. Even out the window . . . Well, no," she admitted. "Not down. I can see up, a little, but down still isn't anything yet. Up it's tomorrow, down it's yesterday. Right?"

"Yes," said Mr. Nicholas.

He had a new trouble. A new embarrassment. For he

A Friend of Mary Rose

needed very much, very suddenly, to get to the bathroom. Was, in fact, going to have to get there—without delay.

He *must* move. He must move, get up, and go back down that hall to the bathroom. Now.

Instead he kept on sitting there. Remembering the time he had heard Dorothea tell his boy how he was—"anyway"—such a clean old man. As if, given the rest of him, she might well have expected him to be dribbling his food, wetting his bed. He had been too amused to be angry. Poor Dorothea, poor Martyr! It must have been a low point for her, that day.

Then, in great haste, he got up.

It startled the child.

"What's the matter?" she said, back to panic. To whispers. "Mister, what—-"

"Nothing." The worst of it was, he had to keep moving as he tried to reassure her. "Stay here. I'm just going to the bathroom."

"But I'll help you! Here—lean—"

"Stay. Here."

He said it between his teeth, and it stopped her. In the interval he got clear out of the room.

Then down the hall. Into the bathroom. Door shut.

His subsequent relief was so great that he was in no way prepared for what happened. In no way capable of defending himself against it, or even of controlling himself. Perhaps he had used up his stock of control.

What he did was to flush the toilet.

The gesture was habitual, he gave it no thought—until

suddenly, washing all thought away in terror, the roaring echoes of that loosed water seemed to dissolve him in despair.

He had given them away. The man would come back. There would be another beating.

For the first time in his life, Mr. Nicholas was lost in absolute physical terror. This had nothing to do with the child, left unprotected behind him. For that moment, for him, there was no child. There was only the lurking man, who would hear—whom he had *summoned*—and his own aching, beaten body.

He would be beaten again.

He could not survive another beating.

How long this madness of terror lasted—for it certainly was nothing else—Mr. Nicholas did not know. When it left him, he found himself half collapsed against the sink, clutching the taps with all his mindless strength.

It was a fortunate position, because he vomited.

Sometime later—again, time unknown—his hands managed to turn the taps. The time that it took to rinse himself, and the sink, and then to capture and feebly suck in some of the water, he was very conscious of. It seemed endless. His clumsiness was past belief. But his mind was his own again.

He was even numbly aware of his fortune in having water. Why had Dorothea not turned this off, too?

At last he was finished, and could allow himself to close the toilet seat and let himself down upon it. With pain and patience, he retrieved his stick from the floor, and crossed his hands on it, and rested.

A Friend of Mary Rose

He felt no shame. His experience did not leave that residue; apparently it was not that kind of experience.

But as feeling did return to him, he found that it was taking the form of anger. Deep, rooted anger, such as he had rarely known—anger quietly and steadily growing in him as he rested there, and giving him something of its own strength, like a miraculous form of nourishment or rest. Anger that he meant to act upon.

When he heard the girl whispering at the door—"Mister! Mister, are you all right?"—he got himself up and answered her calmly.

"Yes, I'm coming."

"Oh, mister, open the door—please! Please come out, please let me help—"

He opened the door. Instantly her little hands were on him, touching, exploring, claiming—but carefully. She remembered to be careful with her hands, though her worrying flowed all over him in words. In whispers.

"Oh, mister, I was so scared—you were so long! I was so scared you passed out or something. . . . Oh, mister, I swear to God, I—"

"Don't say that," said Mr. Nicholas, in his own voice. He added, "It's very rude to call people 'mister.' You must say my name—Mr. Nicholas."

"Yes," she said. "Yes, sure, I know—Mr. Nicholas."

"That's right. Mary Rose."

"Come on," she urged him. "Come back!"

As soon as they were back in his room he heard her turning the key in the lock. (She had trouble with it; no one had turned that lock in years.) So she must have

81

known fear, too, beyond her fear for him. His anger took note of this, as he went back to his radiator cover and let himself down upon it.

The minute he was back in his place, her spirits went up again. This time he wasn't deceived. The fear was still in her, waiting to leap up at any moment—at many moments, perhaps all her life long.

"Oh, now I can see you so *good*," she exclaimed. "All around you—and like where the fences are, out there, and *everything!* What do you think, mister—Mr. Nicholas? Do you think about fifteen more minutes we should go? Do you feel all right? Or half an hour? Where do you have to go?" she said suddenly. "Do you live far, now?"

"Just next door. I'm staying with Mrs. Thompson. Do you know her?"

"Oh, sure, everybody knows her." Her need to be polite made her add: "She's all right, she never reported me."

"Then she knows you, Mary Rose?"

He was only puzzled, that indoor Lettie should know a child he himself could not place; but his question somehow warned her into silence.

He said, "Why are you afraid to tell me your real name, child? You don't think *I'm* going to report you, do you?"

"It's my real name," she said quickly.

He let this pass.

"Do you honestly think I would do anything to make trouble for you, Mary Rose?"

She wanted to answer him, and answer well—the desire brought her closer to him, and she put her hand on his shoulder. Lightly; remembering not to hurt.

But she couldn't find what to say.

"You wouldn't mean to," she said at last.

"I don't do things unless I mean to. I won't make that kind of mistake."

She said shrewdly, "You still want to tell the police, though."

"I'm going to tell the police. I'm going to do everything in my power to see that they find this man who attacked you."

"No, he never did attack me," she said in instant withdrawal. "Mister, don't you ever tell anybody a thing like that because it's a *lie,* he *didn't!* And if you ever even said a thing like that they'd put me in Children's, there wouldn't be anything Bud could do about it, because that's the one thing he—"

"Mary Rose, stop it," he commanded. "This man attacked *both* of us, if you like that better. He beat us up," he said distinctly.

"But you fought him! You fought him *good,* mister—Mr. Nicholas! Boy, I never would have got away if you didn't fight him the way you did—and I would have helped you, if it wasn't for my arm. We could have got him, between the both of us. I never even *thought* you would fight so good!"

He did not say, "I only hung on. I wasn't even trying to fight." The moment when he meant to say it passed—and he let it go. But that small vanity distracted him.

She rushed on, relieved that their difference was over, or that the subject was changed.

"I was the dopey one! Gee, I don't know how he got hold of my arm so fast, though—except it was like I couldn't get it up again, you know? Without I let go my brick, I mean, and I didn't want to do that. But he knocked me loose of it anyway," she admitted. "The thing is, you have to practice on something like that, like hitting down with a brick, because the *brick* makes a difference. You know? It's not like just hitting—it makes your aim different, because of the brick is heavy, like. I should have practiced on it, but I didn't know. I will now, though."

He was not deceived. Under this confident tomboy the frightened child still lay. And he could see no way to learn what he must know without reawakening that child.

He said gravely, "You realize that this man is extremely dangerous, Mary Rose. Especially to you—because you know what he is really like."

"I sure do," she said. "Don't worry—he'll never catch me again!"

"No. We'll make sure of it—that he never again can harm you, or any other child."

Uneasy, she murmured: "He isn't after anybody else. I'm the one he likes. And he won't—"

"*Likes!*" Mr. Nicholas exclaimed.

"No—okay, I didn't mean—I'm the one he's *after,*" she said, despairing. "And I *know* he's a creep, I know it! He's crazy—I wouldn't go anywheres near him again for a million bucks, I'm not even going to make him

A Friend of Mary Rose

sorry, or anything. I'll just keep away from him, I promise!"

Mr. Nicholas said to her, with care: "Tell me this. Do you have any possible reason for shielding this man, aside from not wanting anyone to know what has happened?"

"What?"

"This man, Mary Rose. Is he some—friend of your brother? Or of your father?"

"No!" Shocked, she said, "Gee, that's a lousy thing to say, Mr. Nicholas!"

"I'm sorry. But you don't care what happens to him?"

"No! Why should I care what . . . What do you mean?"

"This is what I mean. If I can have him arrested, and put into jail, without bringing you into it *in any way,* would you be glad?"

"Sure," she said, a minimal agreement. "I guess so. But how could you do that? What could they arrest him for?"

"For what he has done to me," he said quietly. "That will be better than nothing."

In a voice hushed with discovery, she said: "Hey. *Hey!*" she cried. "You could *do* that—sure you could! Why, it could be like he broke into your house—he was going to steal your money! And you caught him, and you had a fight, and he beat you up! You could say like he robbed you, too—boy, then they could really get him. Couldn't they?"

"Yes," he said.

85

Elizabeth Fenwick

"But you ought to get the money out of here first! You could take it away and hide it, before you call the cops—you better do that," she said earnestly. "Do you want me to go up and get it for you? I could, right now—it's getting lighter, I could see up there. And then we could go!"

"But there isn't any money, Mary Rose."

"Oh," she said. And then: "Oh, sure. Okay. It's okay." She didn't believe him. And she was bitterly hurt.

He sighed. His small return of energy was not lasting . . . and there was still so far to go.

Too tired for guile, he murmured, "I'm sorry you believe that story about me. I have many faults, but I'm not a miser."

"I didn't think that! It was just—everybody said—"

"Yes. All right. It doesn't matter. What does matter," he said doggedly, "is that this man should be kept from doing more harm. You want that, don't you?"

"Yes. Sure. Only . . ."

"Only what?"

"Well, how would you know who he was, Mr. Nicholas? I mean, how would you say you knew? If you didn't want to say who told you?"

He recognized the need for care, here, and took time to answer.

"Well, it's this way, child. When you lack one of your senses, then you learn to use your other senses more. They get sharper because they have to. There are many ways in which I recognize people—the way they walk, the way they talk. Even the way they breathe, or the

A Friend of Mary Rose

odors they carry about them. Little habits. My son jingles the change in his pockets, in a certain way. Mrs. Nicholas rubs her fingers together when she is thinking. You snap your socks, don't you?"

She was delighted.

"Hey—that's pretty sharp! I guess I do! Hey, I could practice on that—I could keep my eyes shut like two hours every day, and—"

"But you do understand that I can tell who people are, even though I can't see them?"

"Yes," she said. "Except—you didn't."

He didn't what? Then he understood. The man was someone he ought to have recognized.

"That's true," he said steadily. "But that's because this man was, quite literally, not himself. All the ways in which I would ordinarily have recognized him were changed. His voice, his step. Even his smell. His whole personality. But I *might* have recognized him—no one can prove that I didn't."

"Well . . ."

"Of course they can't. It's a known fact that I can recognize people, Mary Rose. In any ordinary circumstances. And you remember, I am not going to tell how unusual these circumstances were. I shall simply say," he went on, wearily finding words, "that I came upon him here—"

"In the dark! And that was why he didn't see you coming—because you wouldn't *need* any light!"

"Exactly."

"But he didn't know you could tell right away it was

him, in the dark, and so he tried to get away—and he beat you up, and got away!"

"Yes."

Her energy was remorseless. Even the force of her speaking, so close, with her hand upon his shoulder, shook him like a too-powerful motor attached to some ancient chassis.

Then the hand left him.

"He'll tell them it's not true, though. If you tell on him, then he'll tell them I was here."

"He'll be the last one to do that," he said dryly.

"No. He will. He'll say I was here—he'll say it was us that was here, and him that found us. Like when he came upstairs, remember? Remember what he said? That's what he'll tell them."

The panic was back in her voice—so unexpectedly, this time, that he could not adjust to answer it.

He said uncertainly, "No, child, that's not true," and put out his hand. But she eluded it.

"Sure he will—that's what he'll say, if you tell the cops on him. Because if you try to get him in trouble, then he'll try to get us in trouble. Oh, mister—don't!" she burst out. "Please, mister, please—don't tell them!"

He said helplessly, "Mary Rose, you are very wrong about this—now come back here, and don't be so unreasonable."

"But it's not! It's what he'll do, I know he will! You don't know him!"

She said again, but differently, "You don't know him . . ." and he knew she was realizing that this was, literally, true. He did not yet know.

Nor was she going to tell him. The intensity of her silence, the continuing small movements of retreat, told him how narrow she felt her escape had been, from making such a confidence.

He said with a last effort at command: "You are making up things to frighten yourself. This man will be so—"

"No, mister."

Very soft, very final, her breath of answer crossed the room to him. He heard the soft fumbling of the key in the lock.

"What are you doing?" he said sharply. "Mary Rose!"

But he knew what she was doing. She was going away from him—now, quickly, before she could betray herself any more. Or perhaps his mysterious power of recognition, in which he had wanted her to believe, had grown to enormous proportions in her mind: as if he might also have some entry to her thoughts.

She got the key round, and opened the door.

"I'm sorry, mister—I'm sorry—"

He said nothing. She would not have heard him in any case. Her sneakers, that carried so small a weight, rapidly crossed the hall boards and went rushing down the steps. He heard the front doorchain come down, and the door open.

On daylight, he prayed. On clear daylight. The urgency of his hope brought him to his feet once more; and he was crossing the room, doggedly, hopelessly following her, before he realized that he did not even know where she would go.

Chapter Eight

By nine-thirty the next morning, Lettie Thompson had decided to call Dorothea. She got the new number simply by trying the old one, and was rather proud of her efficiency. But at Dorothea's instant response, she got flustered.

"I'm awfully sorry to bother you, dear—but it did seem so odd, that note, I mean. It really frightened me until I looked in and saw him sleeping. But I thought I'd better just tell you, on account of the responsibility. What do you suppose it means?"

"I'll be there in half an hour, Mrs. Thompson," was Dorothea's sole response. So grimly made that Mrs. Thompson began to feel frightened all over again.

The telephone was in the hall, so she had not needed to disturb John to use it. She did risk another peep at him, lying there deeply sleeping on top of the day bed in the daylit room—of course the light would not bother him. But surely he did not usually sleep in his clothing? On top of the covers?

A Friend of Mary Rose

Fear nudged her again, and she tried to slip into the room for a closer look—she wanted to see him *breathe*. But her days for stealthy movement were past, and he heard her—his hand began to grope on the bed beside him. Relieved, she stood still.

He said, "Mary Rose . . ."; but it was a sleeper's voice. She did not reply. When he was still again she got herself out of the room and limped back to the kitchen to wait for Dorothea. She had the note propped up on the table there, so she would not mislay it; but returning, she found it had lost most of its power to unsettle her. It was so clearly untrue, and so clearly—now that she looked at it calmly—the work of a child.

On a child's lined paper, in pencil, someone had painfully written: "Mr. Nicklis is in his house Upstairs. He is hurt very bad."

It was such a queer little message, unlike any child mischief in her experience. Lettie gave a shiver, and put it down again. She felt unexpected concern for the child itself—what confusion had possessed it, to come putting such a note under her door? And so early, too! She hadn't even considered rising to answer the bell at such an hour. The note had lain there a long time, until she did come out to unlock the door and take in her paper. How awful, if its message had been true!

She began to be vaguely sorry she had called Dorothea. Some mystery was here, that she ought to have talked over with John, first. Now perhaps they would both be angry with her—John, and Dorothea too. Well, she couldn't help it.

Yet when Dorothea came—in less than half an hour—Mrs. Thompson's defensiveness died at sight of her. Without makeup, her head wrapped in a plain scarf, Dorothea looked so tired and resigned that Mrs. Thompson's heart went out to her.

"Oh, I shouldn't have bothered you, dear—it's really nothing, and I know how busy you are—"

"No, you were right, Mrs. Thompson," Dorothea said. "I'm the one that's at fault. I knew it all day yesterday, I couldn't sleep last night for thinking about it. Where is Father, please?"

"Why, he's asleep, he's perfectly all right—now at least sit down, dear, and have a little coffee. I've made it fresh for you. And here's this silly note, I don't know why I even paid any attention to it! It's just some child's idea of—something, I don't know."

Dorothea picked up the note and read it standing—read it carefully. Then she put it down, and shook her head. Mrs. Thompson was startled to see tears in her eyes.

"No, it's true—I know it's true. He went over there. And he hurt himself. However he got back here, he's hurt himself. Have you called the doctor?" When Mrs. Thompson stammered that she had not, that such a thing hadn't occurred to her, Dorothea said decisively: "Then I will. May I use your phone?"

At the thought of her rather frightening old friend waking to find himself under medical examination (and through her fault, too) Mrs. Thompson gathered strength to resist.

"Why, I think that would be a mistake, Dorothea—

before you've even looked at him. I've looked at him, and he's—he's just sleeping. He even called me 'Mary' in his sleep—'Mary Rose,' I should say. Though I didn't know he called her that."

"He didn't," said Dorothea flatly. "That wasn't Mother's name. Is he upstairs, Mrs. Thompson?"

"No, no, right in the front room, dear. I don't heat the whole house any more. . . . Right in here, you see. I don't know why he chose not to, not to get ready for bed. I had a pair of George's pajamas laid out for him, but—"

Mrs. Thompson was considerably startled then to have her own sitting-room door closed in her face—with Dorothea on the other side of it. Helpless, she stood there a moment longer and then wandered back to the kitchen and sat down. With relief. Of course Dorothea had not meant to be rude—she was incapable of such a thing. Just overwrought. And to tell the truth, Mrs. Thompson was not anxious to be present when John first woke and found Dorothea poking at him. Let them settle it first, and then she would bring in some nice hot coffee. And the coffeecake that Mr. Rudd had brought down with their chicken yesterday.

Dorothea, alone in the strange parlor, made no attempt to touch her father-in-law. She went and stood over him for some time, noting with exact despair every evidence of disorder and accident that she could find. Nothing surprised her, not his streaked and filthy shirt, nor his torn coat pocket, nor even his visible hand with dried blood on it from some wound. When she came to his head—the poor white hair in such a state as she had

Elizabeth Fenwick

never seen it, the whole side of his face discolored with . . . with dirt? Or bruise?—she paused for a long time.

Then, quietly moving a chair to the day bed, she sat down and put her face in her hands and began—silently, passionately—to cry. This was the one relief that Dorothea allowed herself, and she had learned to do it very quietly. In such a world, and from such a faulty creature as herself, she knew that real grief was not wrong, if it did not call attention to itself or frighten others. That she had never done. And over the years, her occasional crying spells had come to seem a privacy in themselves, where she disturbed no one and no one disturbed her.

Yet all at once he spoke to her.

"What is it? What is it? Where are you, child?"

Immediately, assembling her self-control, Dorothea pulled herself together. She needed a moment before she could speak, and put her hand on his, that seemed to search for her. He took it—seized it—and then grew still.

"What? Dorothea?"

"Yes, Father. I'm here."

He let go of her hand, and began another kind of searching, which she recognized—wanting to know where he was. She told him.

"You're at Mrs. Thompson's, dear. I've come to take you home. How do you feel?"

He didn't reply at once. Then his hand, a little furtively, began exploring himself, his clothing. He wanted to know what she saw. Sadly, she watched him.

"Torn my pocket a bit, haven't I?" he muttered finally.

A Friend of Mary Rose

"It doesn't matter." Unable to bear any more, she said: "You've had a fall, haven't you, dear? I just want the doctor to have a look at you, you won't mind that. To make me feel better."

"Good Lord, what's Lettie told you?" he said—but absently. "Where is she, anyway? What time is it?" Then, canceling these questions in irritation: "Where's my stick?"

She had moved it away, and left it where it was.

"Please don't get up until the doctor's seen you, Father. I don't want to alarm you, but your head—"

"I want to go to the bathroom," he interrupted coldly, and pushed himself up.

She retrieved the stick without further comment. Once—only once—she had tried to bring him a bedpan. He got himself up, struggling against a distress which he could not conceal. Dorothea rose, too, but did not touch him or speak. She saw with a heavy and patient heart that he was going to fall.

He did not. Erratic, staggering a little, he got under way. It was the wrong way; and still in silence, Dorothea walked toward the door. This was the only form of guiding that he permitted, and he turned and followed her. At the door, he put out his hand and found her arm.

"Now stay here, child—don't fuss. Don't worry, I'm all right. I'll be right back."

"I'm going to call the doctor, Father."

"Do as you like."

She turned to the telephone as he reeled into some near-by door. And shut it firmly.

Her own doctor was not available at this hour of the morning, except through messages relayed to the hospital. With no obvious breakage to offer him, she felt shy of making so much trouble—and besides, it would mean delay. After some hesitation, she looked up the number of a semiretired doctor not far away, whom her father-in-law preferred. He was out on neighborhood calls, but his wife promised to find him and send him over. She wanted to know what was wrong with Mr. Nicholas. Dorothea said without expression that he had had a bad fall. Possible concussion. The doctor's wife said, "Oh, dear . . ." and Dorothea cut her off with a polite "Thank you," and hung up.

She did not want to go out into the kitchen, where Mrs. Thompson was hovering in wait, and so pretending to be absorbed in thought she returned to the sitting room and began tidying away all traces of the old man. When this was done she sat down and waited, her dry fingers working upon themselves. He was being very long. She was not going to interfere.

Presently she heard a door open, and her father-in-law's voice saying: "Lettie? Lettie, where are you?"

Had he forgotten she was here, or did he mean to hurt her? Dorothea stayed where she was. She could hear Mrs. Thompson replying, coming to him—trying to urge him into the kitchen. But he did not want that.

"Where's that nice chair I was sitting in last night?" he wanted to know. "I'm a bit turned round, since you changed everything, you know."

They came into the sitting room together, with Mrs. Thompson clumsily attached to him, and he allowing it. Mrs. Thompson gave her an apologetic look, as Dorothea rose in place.

He had done his best to straighten himself up. His face and hands were washed, and his hair was combed, and he had buttoned his jacket over much of the shirt. A button was loose, the torn pocket gaped, and it *was* a bruise on the side of his face. A big one. He looked heartbreaking, and he didn't even know it—Mrs. Thompson was too nervous to mention it. She kept murmuring about coffee.

"Just fresh, and hot. And that coffeecake I showed you last night—"

"I usually take a banana first thing," he replied, "but it doesn't matter. I don't believe I want anything just now, thank you, Lettie. Except to ask you—"

"But Dorothea, you'll have some coffee, won't you?"

He had forgotten her. Unmistakably. Her heart swelled with a kind of bitter pride, to see how startled and guilty he looked. In a low voice, she thanked Mrs. Thompson and refused.

"But I would like to speak to Father a moment, if you don't mind."

Mrs. Thompson, once she grasped what was meant, made a second retreat to her kitchen—urging Dorothea to come and tell her when she wanted coffee. When she had gone, Dorothea came across the room. He still looked disconcerted, but said to her approach: "Well, Dorrie?"

She got down on the floor in front of him, and put her

hands on his knees. Warily, he waited for her to speak.

She said earnestly, "Father, I know what's in your mind. I know you're angry with me, and I deserve it. I was angry with you when I left those pieces—when I planned to leave them! That's why I let Johnny take you away from me. But don't punish me by punishing yourself, dear. Don't do that."

"How do you mean?" he said. And then, "Why didn't you say you didn't like that stuff, Dorrie?"

"I didn't dislike it. It went with the house. But I was worried about fitting it in the new house, and I knew you were upset about moving anyway—and when Mrs. Bohr said how much she wished she had dining-room furniture like that, I—"

"Oh, she's taking it, is she? Well, that's something. I thought you'd left it for the Salvation Army."

"No, dear. I wouldn't have given it to anyone who didn't value it. But you know she's going to have a boarding-house there, and—"

"You gave it to her?"

"Well, sold it. But you know furniture like that doesn't bring a great deal nowadays, Father, and I was afraid you—"

"How much?"

"Well, twenty-five dollars," she said, resigned.

He thought about it.

"I suppose that's a fair price, considering," he said at last. "I can't see why you didn't tell me, though. That's what I minded."

"Because I was a coward," she said at once. "And because I was a coward, I blamed you in my mind for it—I imagined you blaming me, and so I wanted to blame you first. And then it seemed to me I had every right to avoid unpleasantness and just do what was sensible—except that I had to make myself angry at you first, in my mind. So I should have known I was wrong. I was wrong, Father."

"Well, I'm sorry you had such a time of it," he replied.

He sounded a little vague, and she raised her head, noticing how large the bruise looked in this light. It seemed to extend down the whole side of his face. He must have run into something very hard, or else fallen with great force—all alone, miles from her, helpless and deserted. He might well have died at that moment, leaving her to live the rest of her life knowing that he had done so. And why. She put her head down on his knees without a tear. But great pools of tears welled up within her, waiting for solitude.

He put an absent hand on her hair.

"But what did you do with my trunks? I couldn't—"

Chimes interrupted them; and Mrs. Thompson called out from the kitchen: "Oh, Dorothea, would you go?"

"It's Dr. Linen," she said, and got up. "Now, Father—if you forgive me, you must let him see you. If you aren't nice to him, I'll know you mean it for me."

"Good heavens, child, let the man in," he replied.

He listened to hear if she came back, but she was being very scrupulous: only the doctor came into the room, and the door shut behind him. Dorothea's slow steps went on down the hall. Poor Lettie.

"Well, John, you're up, are you?" said Dr. Linen's loud voice. "From what Dorothea said I didn't expect that. Been in a scrap, have you?"

Mr. Nicholas flinched, and said crossly: "Stop that, Roger. Behave like a civilized being. I'm perfectly all right—but as a matter of fact, I'm glad you're here. I think you're the very person . . . What are you doing?"

"You just let me have my innings, here, and then you can have yours," said Dr. Linen. "How did this happen?"

"A little accident," said Mr. Nicholas.

"Is that it? Well, your little accident had shoes, didn't he? Big ones. Let's get you over on this couch, where I can tell what I'm doing. Want help?"

Mr. Nicholas found that he did. Without comment on either side, he was returned to the day bed, and a businesslike silence ensued—broken only by Dr. Linen's "Does this hurt?" and his own "Certainly" or "Certainly not." There were several sharp Certainlies.

Finally Dr. Linen sat back.

"Well, if there's concussion at all, it's very slight," he said. "But I want those ribs X-rayed. An ambulance would be the simplest way to get you there. And it would save trouble all round, of course, if you'd spend a few days at the hospital while we're at it."

"No," said Mr. Nicholas.

Dr. Linen hadn't waited for an answer.

"And you've got a lot of nasty contusions there, as you

know. I don't understand you, John—why don't you want to report this?" he asked. "I'm used to family close-ups, God knows, but that's not your case. Young John could no more do this to you than he could fly, and Dorothea hasn't got the weight. How big is that grandson of yours now?" he asked suddenly.

Mr. Nicholas showed his long teeth.

"Enormous. But we keep him strait-jacketed. Now if you're finished," he said, "I'd like to ask you about a family in this neighborhood. There is a father, ill or otherwise burdensome. A working son named Bud, unmarried. A daughter, probably not named Mary Rose. About eleven or twelve—possibly a small thirteen. Not more."

"Well," said Dr. Linen, and thought. "No idea where, around here?"

"No. Except that the house is probably in considerable disrepair, and there is an automobile that doesn't run standing in the yard."

"Put three or four more in with it, and I'd say Haydens'," said Dr. Linen. "Lord, that place is an eyesore. As a matter of fact, it could be the Haydens," he added. "I don't remember the boy's name, but I suppose he's out of school and working by now. And there was a little girl—Mrs. Reilly on Cross Street used to take her by the day before she went to school. I patched her up a couple of times, haven't seen her since. The father worked for the railroad—engineer, or something. Nothing wrong with him that I know of, except he lost his wife before he got his kids raised."

"Perhaps you are right," Mr. Nicholas said, after a pause. "There aren't many people left around here who occupy a house to themselves. And I have a strong impression that no one else was there."

"When do you mean—when this happened? You were in some strange house when this happened?"

"No, no." Mr. Nicholas's tone became, for him, hesitant. He said, "I would like very much to be sure that the Hayden girl is all right, Roger. Would there be any way of finding that out, without asking directly?"

"You mean of me finding out?" the doctor said bluntly.

"Yes. If they're not your patients, perhaps you might have a patient who's a neighbor? Whom you might drop by to see?"

"Well, what's the point of all this, John—why shouldn't she be all right? I don't like to blunder around completely in the dark, you know."

"No, of course not." Mr. Nicholas hesitated, again, and then apologized for it. "I'm a little tired this morning, I'm afraid. This person who was involved in my accident," he said. "I want to make sure he's done the girl no harm."

"One of her family?"

"No. As a matter of fact, I don't yet know who he is."

"But you mean to find out?"

"If I can. But not at any cost to the girl. Mainly, I want to be sure that she is at home, and all right."

Dr. Linen said as he rose: "This sounds to me like a small part of an ugly story, John."

"Yes. I'm sorry I can't be more help. If the brother's name were Bud," he said, "you could be sure it's the right girl. Perhaps you could find out her name for me."

"Well, the Millers next door to them are patients of mine," the doctor began, when the old man interrupted with a sharp cry.

"Then it's Mary Rose! How stupid of me, I knew that there were neighbors named Miller. I think my mind must be going," he said, exasperated.

"I shouldn't be surprised, the way you treat it. All right; then I'm definitely interested in the Hayden girl, am I? To see if she's home, and all right."

"If you can—indirectly, Roger, please. I gather that the two families aren't on very good terms."

"All the better. People can't wait to talk about their enemies. Well, all right," he said. "I'll have the ambulance round for you within the hour—I can call from here. And I'll come tell you what I can, as soon as I can. At the hospital, that is."

An awful silence followed him. He turned at the door, to enjoy it.

Mr. Nicholas said with restraint, "I think it would be wrong to worry Dorothea that way, Roger. If I were kept at the hospital, she would assume that my injuries were serious."

"They are, at your age," said the doctor. "And if you want to bring Dorothea into it, how's she going to manage you and a new house at the same time?"

"I don't need to be managed. I'm perfectly capable—"

"You're perfectly capable of going out and getting into more trouble. Now fair's fair, John," he said firmly. "If I've got to run mysterious errands for you, I want you off my mind while I'm doing it. And don't worry about Dorothea, I'll talk to her."

"You talk to the Millers," said Mr. Nicholas bitterly. "And just overnight, mind you—that's the absolute limit."

Dr. Linen didn't even bother to reply.

Chapter Nine

It was night before Mr. Nicholas had any profit from his bargain, but the profit was considerable when it came.

Meanwhile he underwent exactly the dehumanizing process he had foreseen: was delivered, handled, dulled, manhandled, and stashed away in smelly, echoing solitude. He did not get the particular strong-minded type of nurse who found his independence an offense and set out to quash it—no, his was sweet, with cloying hands, and thought he was cute. He also had a maddening harness round his middle, and bedpans.

Dr. Linen showed up after dinner, the easy author of all this humiliation. Mr. Nicholas forced himself to civil replies, and waited.

"Well, I saw your girl," the doctor said, after minimum preliminaries—he was a fair man. "You're a fine pair, you are. That fellow must be marked up, too, you know—ever thought of that?"

"You saw Mary Rose? She's hurt?"

"There is no Mary Rose, forget that. Your cherub is

Mickey Hayden, the terror of the block—according to Mrs. Miller. She's eleven, she looks like an undersized jockey, and I doubt if there's much about this world she doesn't know. That's not worth knowing," he amended. "I wish you'd tell me what this is all about!"

"Is she hurt?" said Mr. Nicholas patiently.

"Well, she's been in a scrap, and looks it. In fact, she's confined to quarters for fighting—her old man yelled out the window at her while she was talking to me, and she skedaddled back inside. So you won't have to worry about her getting into any more trouble for a while—the block's safe from both of you," he said.

"How did you come to talk to her? What did she say?"

"Well, she was waiting for me when I came out of the Millers'—hanging around behind the bushes between the yards. I didn't even see her, just heard somebody whispering 'Mister, mister' in the bushes, and there she was—glaring up at me like some little one-eyed wild creature. She's got a lovely shiner. Pain?" he asked, to Mr. Nicholas's checked sigh.

"No."

"I held up your dope, so you can hear all this good news. There isn't much more. She wanted to know what happened to the old man that the ambulance took away. I asked her why she wanted to know, and that threw her. I said, 'Do you know him?' and she looked as if she couldn't remember the Fifth Amendment. Then all of a sudden she got brave and said, 'Yes! He's Mr. Nicholas!' So I told her you were all right, and just needed a few days' rest—and that if she was a friend of yours she could come and see you here, after tomorrow. How's that?"

"What did she say?"

"Said she couldn't. Got in a fight, and was being punished. But would I tell you hello? I said, 'Who from?' but she couldn't think of the answer to that one, either. Then the old man yelled at her, and she said very fast, 'Tell him love from Mary Rose—that's another girl, he knows her.' And that was that. She holds her arm wrong when she runs," he added. "Something happened to that, too."

"I wish you could have looked at it," said Mr. Nicholas. "Although I can't believe they seriously neglect the child. . . . What did the Millers say?"

"Mrs. Miller," the doctor corrected. "I don't think I'll bother to repeat it, she doesn't seem sane on the subject. All I had to do was glance out the window and remark on the cars in the yard next door, and her beloved hemorrhoids went right down the drain. The boy is a gangster, with gangster pals, the child is a vicious delinquent, the father is a whisky soaked bum, and they all ought to be forcibly removed from Mrs. Miller's vicinity. Would be, if she could manage it."

"I see," said Mr. Nicholas. "No, I don't think Mrs. Miller is much use to us. We'll have to try someone else."

"You mean I will," said Dr. Linen. "By the way, I ordered that bedpan—I consider it necessary for a time. I wouldn't like to think you were refusing it."

"I haven't much choice, have I?" said Mr. Nicholas mildly. "What about the Rudds, at the corner store? They deal with everyone round there."

"I'm ahead of you. I went there. I don't care much for

them," he said frankly. "They're too damned obsequious—makes me feel like a brute, or a health inspector. I bet she could be a devil, too, without much trying. However. At least she could tell me the facts—which I had forgotten, or didn't know. It seems that shortly after Hayden's wife died he did begin to hit the bottle, and one day while under the influence he ran his train past some stop signal and hit another train. Nobody killed, but several people injured, and lots of damage. And that was the end of him with the railroad. Pretty much the end of him as a man, too—he didn't know any other trade, and was too old to learn one. The boy went right to work out of high school, seems to be a hard worker and a good car mechanic, or whatever they call them. I have a feeling he's good-looking, too—Mrs. Rudd talks about him very indulgently. And she's sorry for the father. Got no use for the girl, though—she's a bad one."

Mr. Nicholas said, "And did she strike you as a bad one, Roger?"

"Well, she's a wild one—no doubt about that. In fact, the whole family sounds like something out of the backwoods—clannish, touchy, hot-tempered. Hard up. One fellow swears the old man keeps a shotgun handy, but I wouldn't take that too seriously."

"What do you mean, one fellow? You've asked other people about them?"

"Oh, here and there. You've got me intrigued, you know. But don't worry, I've got the perfect opener—all I have to do is mention that yard full of cars, and I hear all about the terrible Haydens. Wouldn't think a place

A Friend of Mary Rose

like DeKuyper Street would be so sensitive to a few junk cars in somebody's yard, would you? Considering all the ones along the curb. Well, have you got enough to sleep on tonight?" he asked. "You've got to face Dorothea tomorrow, you know. I hadn't the heart to keep her out another day."

"Yes, all right," said Mr. Nicholas absently.

But Dr. Linen, perhaps against his own judgment, still lingered. An active and vigorous man in his sixties, warned into semiretirement by a heart attack, he found himself these days with not enough life to satisfy a lively temperament. And reticence teased him.

"What do you think of your Mary Rose now?" he said curiously. "Still think you should have got mixed up in her battles?"

"I think so. This one."

"Well, I'll say one thing—whatever she did, that was a damned vicious brute that attacked you both. It wasn't Miller was it?" he said suddenly.

"I've told you, Roger—I don't know."

"Yes. I remember. Well, let me know when you get ready to find out," he said, half joking. "I seem to have unsuspected talents in the detective line. Only don't wait till his bruises fade!"

When he had gone, Mr. Nicholas felt an ungrateful relief. The information his friend had brought him was useful, he was glad to have it—but the grotesque, almost caricatured view Dr. Linen had presented of Mary Rose and her family had begun to tire him. He understood that the Haydens now offered this view of themselves to the

109

world—indeed, forced it, with their stubborn junk yard, their feuds, and probably their careless appearances. They were responding with defiance to their difficulties and ill-luck, no doubt, and increasing both with every gesture. But this was the outside view of them. Necessary to be aware of, perhaps, but bearing about as much relation to Mary Rose and her brother and father as did the crabby old attic miser to Mr. Nicholas himself. No; he had needed to know about Mary Rose, in order not to lose her. But to know her, that was a matter between Mary Rose and himself.

The loneliness of the child appalled him. To be in such danger as she had been in, and to fear every authority to whom she might turn for help! The police, her brother, the neighbors—even, in the end, himself. And yet in this forest of fears she was living almost jauntily—"practicing on" her brick-swinging, and on other fierce accomplishments, he supposed. Observing her world with inventiveness, and even delight. Prepared to cope singlehanded with her enemies, so long as she could, whether they were an irate neighbor-woman or a lethal madman. For Mr. Nicholas had no doubt that Mary Rose would have died in that attic, if things had gone otherwise.

"What did you say?" said the nurse.

He hadn't even heard her come in.

"I don't want that," he said, fussed. Meaning, Go away.

"Don't want what?" she said, taking his arm. He withdrew it at once.

"That injection. It's not necessary."

"Yes it is. You don't want to be in pain all night, do you?"

"I want the use of my mind. If the price of that is some pain, I'm quite willing to pay it."

"The use of your mind!"

This wasn't the one who thought he was cute. This one thought he was mad.

"You've got plenty of nights to use your mind," she said finally. "This one you need to sleep."

"I haven't got plenty of nights left for anything," he retorted, "and it's my business how I spend them. Now go away!"

She said she would have to report him, but she went.

Of course he then began to mind the harness a great deal—he had been much better off without it, in the first place. Besides, she had broken his train of thought, leaving in him some mounting sense of urgency for which he could not account. About Mary Rose . . . but what? She was home, she was being closely watched (for whatever reason). She was not hurt, in any grave sense. And she knew her enemy now, he could not surprise her again.

But did she know him to be a *mortal* enemy? Did she fear him *enough?* Did she realize what extreme cause she had to fear this man—*and he to fear her?*

For how could he ever be assured that she would not tell? If not at once—and he knew by now that she had not told at once—then eventually. He would not dare to trust her with so terrible a secret as his other identity.

The back door didn't lock.

Mr. Nicholas began to doubt his own sanity.

Why was he lying here, keeping this man's secret for him? What possible choice could there be between some mild discomfort for Mary Rose and her very life? He could not understand why it had even mattered to him that he did not know the man's name—he knew and could testify absolutely to his existence, to his mad behavior, to his victim; and once this much was known, and Mary Rose questioned, why should she keep back his name?

Except that she would deny everything. He could hear her doing it. Would deny everything, including him, and turn to fight him as relentlessly as she fought Mrs. Miller, or any other who wanted to get her "put into Children's."

Well, he could accept that. But what *was* "Children's"? Children's Court? Children's Home? Children's Protective something-or-other? He had a shrewd idea that Mary Rose's picture of some ravening institution, lying in wait to snatch her, must be pure fiction. Surely so long as any family group could manage without becoming a public charge, or a public nuisance, no one wanted to interfere with them.

Was Mary Rose a public nuisance?

Or could Bud abandon them, if he became sufficiently "fed up"?

Mr. Nicholas saw that he could no longer answer his own questions. He knew little of legal matters. In a long and rather autocratic career as a frame maker, without peer in his craft, and accustomed to making his own terms with museums and collectors alike, Mr. Nicholas had done almost no litigating. His private affairs he had

A Friend of Mary Rose

simply turned over to an old friend who happened to be a lawyer. About municipal facilities, for those who needed them, he knew next to nothing; and about family responsibilities as laid down by law, nothing at all.

But at least his puzzling had quieted down that echo of last night's panic (for that was what it had been). Mary Rose was not safe, in any way. But he had no real doubt that she was safe for the night.

Mr. Nicholas rang his bell.

When it was answered—not very soon—he said: "I think I should like that injection now, nurse. I'm sorry I was sharp with you."

"I thought you'd change your mind," she said briefly. "Through using it, are you?"

"Yes. Or rather, I'd like to be."

"Wouldn't we all?" she said mysteriously, and pushed up his sleeve.

Chapter Ten

John was a good son, if a little too easygoing (he had his mother's nature), and he showed no annoyance with his father next morning. Probably he felt none. Even his father's obstinate dismissal of what had happened to him as a "slight accident" failed to exasperate him, although clearly Dorothea had charged him to get the details. His father wasn't going to give them; and after a short struggle he gave up, and accepted this.

Mr. Nicholas then thought it fair to point out to John some other reasons why he, John, might be expected to feel annoyed.

"I'm sorry to cause all this inconvenience just when we're moving, John. And to take you away from your work, too."

"It should happen oftener," John said. "Skipping the office, I mean."

He had been employed for many years in the drafting department of a large engineering corporation. He seemed safely niched there, and fairly content. It was not

A Friend of Mary Rose

Mr. Nicholas's idea of a career, but he knew that times had changed.

"I hope Dorothea didn't mind your coming alone."

"No, afternoon's better for her anyway. How long are they going to keep you here, Dad? It's not like anything was broken, is it? I should think you'd be just as well off at home."

"Why? The expense is going to be negligible, with my insurance. And it gives Dorothea a chance to settle."

"Yes, but she doesn't. She won't, till she gets you back under her eye. And don't tell me you like this! I think you'd both be a lot better off if you came home. You'll like the house—your bathroom's like Florida."

Mr. Nicholas was touched, but wary.

"Well, we'll see," he said. "I'll talk to Dorrie. But there are a couple of things I want to talk over with you, first. I wish you would ask Mr. Marks to come and see me, Johnny. We should get the date for the closing put up. Mrs. Bohr doesn't need all this time, we can make some other arrangement. The main thing is that we should get the money, or whatever it is, transferred over. Do you realize how awkward it would have been for you if this—business had finished me? That house, and the sale price we'll realize from it, are still in my name—and the new title is in yours. We don't want a lot of probate delays in between. You tell Mr. Marks what our problem is, and ask him to come talk to me. Will you?"

"Yes," said John. He added: "You feeling mortal this morning, Dad?"

Elizabeth Fenwick

"I'm feeling sensible, and about time, too. We should have done something about this years ago."

"Well, we tried, didn't we? It's not the world's easiest job to sell a house on DeKuyper Street. For a decent price."

"Then I should have put it in your name," said his father. "Well. Enough hindsight. But get hold of Mr. Marks."

John said he would. He sounded depressed; he had never liked coping with money problems. Neither did Mr. Nicholas. But he could think of no other excuse for summoning his lawyer. Besides, the problem was quite real.

"Well," he said, dismissing it, "now I have a favor to ask you. You know the Haydens, up on the corner?"

"I know who you mean. That beat-up place with all the junk cars in the yard. I think they lost us a couple of chances to sell."

"Yes. Now the boy is a mechanic, I think, in some garage or filling station. Probably in the neighborhood. You wouldn't know which one it might be?"

"Gosh, no, Dad. I wouldn't know him if I saw him. Why?"

"I'd like to talk to him, and I don't want to approach him at home. I wonder how we could find out where he works?"

"Well, I don't know—I could ask around, I guess. But why? What do you want to talk to him about?"

"About his sister," said Mr. Nicholas, who had thought

116

this out. "One of the little girls on the block. I have reason to believe she may be in some trouble, and I think he ought to be warned, to help her. They're not a very popular family locally—there's no mother, and the father drinks. I suppose the children run rather wild. And yet they're not bad people, you know. It seemed to me that I might be able to talk to the boy, as another old resident. Like his own people."

This had seemed to Mr. Nicholas, when he arranged it, a very good explanation. He couldn't imagine why Johnny just sat there in silence.

"Well?" he said—and heard his son move.

"Why—yes, Dad, I see. But—you want this fellow to come over and talk to you? About his sister?"

"Certainly. If he will."

More silence. What was wrong?

"What's wrong?" he said impatiently.

"Nothing—nothing. I just don't understand it. You've never gotten mixed up in neighborhood stuff before."

Too late, Mr. Nicholas recognized the justice of this. The fault was not in his story; it was in himself.

"Well, not for many years," he said weakly. It was all he could think of to say.

"Is this something Mrs. Thompson's put you up to?"

Mr. Nicholas's temptation was brief, and he won.

"Of course not."

John, however, marked the hesitation, and so discounted the reply.

"Well, all right. I don't suppose it can do any harm, if you really want to do it. After all, you won't be around there any more. In case the guy resents it, or something."

"I'm not going to cause any resentment," his father said. "And by the way, John, I wish you could find time to stop by and apologize to Mrs. Thompson. For me. I didn't intend to let her in for so much bother. Perhaps you could take her some flowers."

John said he would. He said, "I'll go by the old neighborhood, and see what I can find out for you, and then I'll go on down and see Joe Marks. I suppose I could ask the Rudds about this fellow. They seem to know everything about everyone."

"You call Mr. Marks 'Joe'?" said his father.

"Sure. Everybody does."

"But he's many years your senior, John."

This made his son laugh—that bright burst of pure enjoyment which occasionally escaped him, and which neither Dorothea nor his father could resist. If he had been a calculating man, he could have got away with almost anything at home. Except, his father felt sure, no calculating man could laugh that way.

"It's true," said Mr. Nicholas, sticking to the point.

"Sure, I know. So does Joe. But you better not remind him."

"And about the Rudds—isn't there someone else you could ask? Dr. Linen has already picked up a point or two from them, and I think it would be better to spread things out more."

"A point or two? About the Haydens? Look," said John, "just what are you up to, Dad?"

Luckily, Mr. Nicholas had an idea just then.

A Friend of Mary Rose

"Actually, we may be able to find out what we need to know by telephoning," he said, and groped on his table. "Here—let me see if I can get a number for them. The Haydens. Then you can simply ask where to get in touch with the boy—his name is Bud. As if you had a car to be fixed, or something of that sort. You needn't give your name," he added.

"I gathered that," said John dryly.

Mr. Nicholas, after some polite negotiation with the hospital switchboard, was able presently to hand John a receiver already registering ringing. John took it hastily, clearing his throat, but several more rings went by before a sharp male voice answered.

"Yes? Who's this?"

"Is Bud there?"

"Bud? No, he don't get home till round six-thirty. Who's this?"

"Where could I reach him? It's about a car," said John.

"Well, you can get him at the station, I guess. You know the number?" John said he didn't, and wrote down the number he was given. Then he asked, "Where is the station?"

This was a mistake. The voice sharpened again.

"What? Say, who is this?"

"Never mind," John said hastily, "I guess I can find it. Thanks."

Anxiously following this, his father demanded: "What's the matter? Wouldn't he tell you?"

"Wanted to know who I was. If you know Bud, apparently you know the station. Never mind, it's simpler just to call the station and ask where they are."

"Well, as a matter of fact, John," his father said, "there's no reason I can't call this boy up myself. I don't know why I didn't think of this before," he added, vexed with himself. "It seems to be possible to do everything over the telephone nowadays. I rarely used it, myself."

"I remember," said John; and his father heard him smiling. "When they did call you up, they used to say: 'Do you think Mr. Nicholas would come to the telephone?' Boy, you really had it made, Dad."

There was pride in his voice, not a trace of envy—a selflessness that Mr. Nicholas did not find entirely comforting.

"Well, those were different times," he said glumly. "I suppose I could call Mr. Marks up, too, couldn't I? So it seems I've bothered you for nothing, Johnny."

"So you have. You can even call up the florist, for Mrs. Thompson's flowers, can't you?"

But he was teasing, he knew better. His father replied only: "Perhaps you'd better get her something in a pot, in case she feels the way Dorrie does about buying cut flowers. And please express my thanks to her, for a most enjoyable stay."

"I'll also suggest she do her own dirty work from now on," said John.

Since his father was clearly not going to do any telephoning until he left, John left. He would have given a good deal to hear Mr. Nicholas's end of the conversation

A Friend of Mary Rose

with Bud Hayden—and a good deal more to hear both sides.

Mr. Nicholas, intent simply on the mechanics of reaching Mary Rose's brother, had no time to worry about other aspects. John had told him the number, and had also rewritten it heavily, in case he forgot. Just the same he was relieved to be answered by someone who said: "Al's Service Station."

"Good," said Mr. Nicholas. "Now—is there a Mr. Bud Hayden employed there?"

"This is Bud."

"Excellent. Now, Bud, this is Mr. Nicholas, of 143 DeKuyper Street. Do you know who I am?"

"Yes," said Bud. "Sure. You just moved, didn't you?"

"That's right. I'm now calling you from United Hospital, where I am spending a few days. I'm sorry to disturb you at your work, but I wonder if you could come by and talk to me for a short while, sometime today. Do you think you could manage that? It's important, of course, or I shouldn't ask you. Important to you as well as to me."

Bud said, "Was it you that called my old man just now?"

What a beleaguered family, Mr. Nicholas thought. The father at once needing to report so small a strangeness!

"Yes, it was I. Or rather, someone calling for me. I didn't know where to reach you during the daytime, you see. Now, if you could come—"

"Well, just what would this be about, Mr. Nicholas?"

Bud's voice broke in with impatience, or nervous irritation—controlled, though, for so young a voice. Nor was there any intentional rudeness in it. "Is it a car, or what?"

"No, no—I'm afraid we were trying not to alarm your family—not very successfully. No, I want to talk to you about your sister. Rather urgently, in fact."

"About Mickey? What about Mickey?" The question was flatly asked; those controls had tightened, Mr. Nicholas was sorry to hear. "You got some complaint about her, mister?"

"No, I have not. On the contrary," said Mr. Nicholas, with an emphatic wish to reassure. "Entirely to the contrary. I have her welfare very much in mind, and that is why—"

"Well, I tell you how it is, Mr. Nicholas. We're pretty busy here right now, and I wouldn't be able to get away. You say you got no complaint about the kid—right? So maybe I could give you a ring about this sometime later. All right?"

It wasn't in the least all right. The instant evaporation of interest from Bud's voice was startling. If it wasn't a complaint, he didn't care what it was. Only a thread of minimal politeness held him there at all, with his real interest already returned to the clamor in his background.

Mr. Nicholas swallowed his indignation—or most of it.

"No, Bud, that is not all right. What I have to say to you about Mary Rose is both urgent and important, and—"

"*Mary Rose?*" The boy's attention was back, sharply.

A Friend of Mary Rose

Then: "How come you call her Mary Rose?" he asked, clearly entertained.

"Because I was told that was her name. Isn't it?"

"Well, sure—but you better not call her by it! I didn't think there was anybody around that remembered, even."

He sounded almost friendly. Encouraged, Mr. Nicholas said: "Oh, yes. Mary Rose remembers."

"You mean she *told* you that was her name?"

"Of course." In the small succeeding pause, Mr. Nicholas added: "I can't tell you how important it is that you find some time to come and talk to me, Bud. I would come to you if I could, but that isn't possible. It isn't more than a fifteen-minute drive, is it?"

"No, I guess not." With sudden decisiveness, he said: "Maybe I could drop by on my lunch hour, but it would have to be fast. You care if I bring my lunch?"

"Bring it by all means. And come directly to my room—it's 214. In the left wing."

"Okay, 214 in the left wing. I'll see you around quarter past twelve then, okay?"

"Yes. Thank you," said Mr. Nicholas.

He was invaded by a sadness that he did not understand, after he had hung up. Quite suddenly, like some emotion remembered from another time of life, sadness came down upon him. He lay quietly, not attempting to reason it away, and it turned into sleep.

He was wakened by his lunch, which meant that Bud would be coming soon. The sadness was gone. He remembered, and sensed for it, like a presence in the room; but it was gone.

The lunch, however, was there—and his "cute" nurse, who still hoped to feed it to him. To save time, he allowed this, and they finished up rapidly. He then boldly proposed that coffee and cake should be brought to his room for a friend. She gave in so easily he was sorry he had not asked for another lunch.

Bud was a little late. He was also, Mr. Nicholas became aware, sorry he had come. And intending to leave as soon as possible.

But he had felt obliged to keep his word and come. That was something.

Mr. Nicholas struck for his attention firmly, and at once.

"First, Bud, I want to tell you something I haven't been able to tell Mary Rose—how much I admire the courage, and generosity, and strength of character she showed me at a time when there was no obligation whatsoever. And nothing possible to be gained by it. It was simply an expression of her true character—and I hope that you know it's a fine one. A very fine one."

Bud, having declined to sit down, heard this standing by the bed. He was entirely silent.

"You don't underestimate your sister, I hope, because she's a child?"

"Mick's a good kid. Nobody has to tell me that."

"She's much more than a good kid," said Mr. Nicholas severely. "She is a most unusual person, both in character and intelligence. And more than that, Mary Rose has a loving heart. The rest would be meaningless without that."

A Friend of Mary Rose

A sudden sound escaped the young man standing beside him. It took the form of a laugh, an uncertain and explosive laugh—but it was an involuntary escape of voice, Mr. Nicholas felt, and might have taken any form. Bud covered it by an immediate noisy adjustment of his chair, and by sitting down.

He said then, "It really hits me, the way you keep on calling her 'Mary Rose'! You don't know how weird that sounds."

"They gave me some coffee for you," Mr. Nicholas replied. "Can you see it? Would you like some?"

"Yes, sure," said Bud. "Thanks." He didn't move, though, nor did Mr. Nicholas interrupt his tense silence.

It broke again, with the same abruptness.

"God, you don't know what it's like, to hear somebody say something decent about the kid! Just once, just something!" Now he was leaning forward, his restlessness jarring Mr. Nicholas's bed. "Sure I know she's bright—I knew it a long time before they did, with their crappy tests and all. And you know something? When they found it out, that was just something else to hit her with! 'Potential,' " he said bitterly. "Boy, that's a word I'd like to take, I'd like to ram it. . . . It's like they want to punish her, for being smart. You know? If she was some rich kid, okay, it would all be roses. They could believe it, then! But some poor little snot-nose mick, what right has she got to be a genius? It's like, if she is one, then they got to prove she's a bad one—you know? Otherwise the whole system don't work!"

He had let out too much hostility, there was no place

to use it in this quiet room. The tail of it swung round on Mr. Nicholas.

"So how come you know so much about her?" he demanded. "And what's this 'Mary Rose' bit, anyway? Just when did she tell you about that?"

Mr. Nicholas answered carefully.

"Night before last, Bud. When we were both hurt. Her 'fight' was actually an attempt to help me, in great part. I'm not supposed to tell you this, of course."

"Yeah," he said, intent. "I can believe it. That's another thing—all of a sudden I'm not supposed to know anything any more. So what happened?" But before Mr. Nicholas could begin to reply, Bud swept past his own question. "You see how it is? Now I got to go ask around, I want to know what's happening in my own family! Or else stand there while some creep gives me a long story, I don't know what they're talking about. Not you, mister— I don't mean that. Believe me, they're not all like you! Even the ones that start out nice, like what a bright little girl she is—boy, they are the worst. I *know* she's bright," he said with passion. "I *know* she's a little girl—I know she ought to have a nice home, and a nice mama and papa, and pretty stuff to wear—she's the one that don't know it! You know that? You know what's in that kid's closet right now, she won't even look at it? Not any junky stuff—I got a friend that knows exactly what girls ought to wear, she's got very good taste. Well, I gave her fifty dollars to get Easter stuff for that kid—fifty bucks, that's not raisins, right? And she got it. Everything. The best. So where is it? Did she ever wear it—did she ever even put it on? You just guess, mister. Just take one guess."

Mr. Nicholas sighed.

"Well, there's no doubt it's a considerable burden for a man, to bring up a little girl."

"Listen, she's no burden to me, she's my sister—I'm not complaining! All I'm saying is—"

"Oh, a boy would have been far easier, Bud. A younger brother. There's no harm in admitting that. And surely you see that Mary Rose figured it out long ago."

"How do you mean?"

"Well, how does she come to call herself 'Mickey'?" he asked.

Bud said quickly, "She didn't call herself 'Mickey,' it's her nickname. We always called her that."

"When your mother was alive?"

Bud now discovered the coffee Thermos. Mr. Nicholas heard him fiddling with it, before he asked: "Sure it's okay if I drink some of this?"

"Yes, it's for you. Please have your lunch. I've had mine."

"Oh, I left that in the car. It's okay."

At least he wasn't troubling to disguise his former intentions. Mr. Nicholas drew faint hope from this, and waited. Bud also found the cake.

"As a matter of fact, I can tell you exactly how that got started," he said presently, munching. "She didn't have a thing to do with it. There was this old biddy used to take care of her in the daytime, when Dad was working—I still went to school. Well, she meant well—I guess she was kind of a nice old biddy, but she used to make this big thing of it every time Mick fell down, or something—call the doctor, and she was always plastering stuff all over her. A real fusser. Well, we didn't want to hurt her feelings, but finally my dad did say she shouldn't worry so much. You know, she might make the kid nervous, or something. So he just told her, like a joke, he said, 'Hell, she's a little mick, they're tough, you can't hurt a mick.' So Mi—so my sister naturally says, 'What's a mick?' and Dad says, 'You're a mick, that's what, and don't forget it!' "

It was a pleasant recollection. Mr. Nicholas could hear him smiling as he recalled it. Or perhaps a pleasant time to recollect, when he had still been a boy, and his father had still done a man's work, and they had lived a fairly normal life.

Before he had got so fed up.

Chapter Eleven

The empathy between Mary Rose and himself, so briefly and deeply established in his empty house, persisted in curious ways still, Mr. Nicholas found. One was in the flurry of panic that could rise in him all at once—like hers, absolutely resistant to reason—in which her violent destruction seemed both certain and imminent. As, indeed, it had nearly been. He felt sure these echoes of their common terror still rose in her, and even wondered if they happened at the same time as his—Mr. Nicholas was not averse to wonders.

Another persistence lay, he now realized, in his attitude to Bud. He knew perfectly well that Bud was not really the arbiter of anyone's fate. But to Mary Rose, he was—and this emotional aura hung round him and hampered Mr. Nicholas in speaking out.

Both these remnants of empathy hampered him. He needed a clear mind to realize just what Mary Rose's situation was, and to take steps to correct it. The main trouble was that her immediate danger was so bound up with her precarious family life that Mr. Nicholas did not know how to protect her from the one without destroying the other. He preferred to begin with Bud, but he did not know if Bud was capable of hearing what had really happened without losing his head and rushing into disastrous action.

Certainly the boy was too tightly wound up, too nervously guarded, for his years. His feeling for his sister seemed genuine, but confused. Where the father came in was another blank—except that his misfortunes seemed to have turned him almost paranoid. On the whole, Mr. Nicholas felt the need for great care.

Bud, having gulped down his cake and coffee, now wanted a cigarette—and remembered to ask.

"Okay to smoke in here, Mr. Nicholas?"

"Perfectly, Bud. Is there an ash tray?"

"I can use the cup. I guess you don't smoke, right? Is that on account of, uh, you don't see?"

"Yes, it is. You've heard of that, have you?"

"Oh, sure. At first it sounds nuts, but all you got to do is try it in the dark sometime—I mean real dark. It's no good. Funny, isn't it?"

This was such a poignant echo of Mary Rose that Mr. Nicholas's caution melted.

He said, "I'm extremely glad you came, Bud. I appreciate it. Your sister's been much on my mind."

"Well, she's on mine, too, believe me. Only most people that want to talk to me about her, well, they don't really like her. You know? That's no good."

"No."

A Friend of Mary Rose

"I mean, I can tell you like the kid."

It was a kind of question, and Mr. Nicholas answered emphatically.

"Very much indeed."

"Yeah. I could tell."

He was savoring this. Mr. Nicholas decided to risk the moment.

"What particularly worries me is that I'm afraid she may have made an enemy, in our—our difficulties the other night," he said. "Even a dangerous enemy."

"Who?" Bud said sharply.

"Well, that's it. I don't know who this man is."

"What man? What do you mean," he said suddenly, "some *man* beat her up like that? It wasn't kids?"

"Oh, no, it wasn't kids. This was a man of, I should say, forty to fifty, perhaps older. A heavy-set man, with a good head of hair. A beer drinker."

"Miller," said Bud. His chair scraped back violently. "By God, that's Miller. I'll kill him. I'll kill him. . . ."

"Now, just a minute. Bud! Listen to me. I don't think it was Miller."

Bud came back, but altered.

"What do you mean, you don't think it was Miller? You said you didn't know who it was. So how do you know it's not Miller all of a sudden?"

"I don't, of course. But from something Mary Rose said, I doubt it very much. Besides, however unpleasant your neighbor may be, he isn't a criminal lunatic, is he? This man is, I can assure you."

Bud said, almost in a whisper, "Oh, Christ—what are

131

you talking about? You lie there—you lie there talking—"

"I'm lying here because I also got in his way," said Mr. Nicholas. "Fortunately I'm out of it now. Mary Rose isn't. Will you let me tell you about it?"

For a moment Bud didn't speak. Then, in his original tight voice, he replied: "I guess I'll let my sister tell me, thanks. That'll be a straight story, at least."

"It'll be a story, I can promise you that," said Mr. Nicholas. "You don't get truth from anybody when you behave as you're doing, at the first hint of it. Go home and make a fine scene—she expects you to. That's why she doesn't tell you things any more."

"I guess I'm pretty sick of you telling me about my own sister, too—how come you're in the middle, all at once? You get her into bad trouble—you get her into some mess she don't even dare tell me about, and then you lie here and talk like you're the only person in the world can handle Mick. Mary Rose!" he said, with savage contempt. "Giving me all that crap about the kid—what was that for? To soften me up, so I wouldn't get sore you nearly got her beat to death? What kind of an old guy are you, anyway—hiding behind a kid?"

Mr. Nicholas said steadily, "I was not able to protect Mary Rose, that's true. I'm not able to now. I had hoped you might be able to—she needs protection, and she needs it badly. Go do what you like, and think what you like, but remember that—your sister needs all your protection."

The boy above him was a hard breathing—nothing

A Friend of Mary Rose

more. Then, with a muttered word, he turned and slammed out of the room—became a pounding of hard soles down the hospital corridor. And then nothing.

Mr. Nicholas had failed. Worse, he had brought Mary Rose's affairs to the crisis she most dreaded—and at a time when she had already borne more than a child should bear. It was worse than failure, it was disaster.

And he was too angry to care.

He was so angry, in fact, that his anger affected him like a tonic. A freedom. For what had failed was his last attempt to follow Mary Rose's way—a child's way, in a world of total enmity and one shaky refuge. Which was no refuge at all. He had known better all along. Now he would act as he should have acted from the beginning, like a sane adult, a citizen of a sane adult world. Instead of a cautious intermediary between two madmen! Because the father was as mad in his way as that devil in the attic, and he had already infected the son. What if she did lose a home like that? She was better off without it!

His "cute" nurse had come in, indignant—was checking his pulse, his skin, clucking all over him. He barely noticed. The first thing was Marks. To call Joe Marks. Then . . .

His nurse gave a cry, and rose.

"You get out of here, young man! Don't you dare come in this room!"

"That's for him to say. Let him say it," said Bud's tight voice, from the door.

"If you don't leave this—"

"Just a minute, nurse. What is it you want?" Mr.

Nicholas demanded, turning his face toward the door.

"You know what I want. I want to know what trouble the kid's in—and that's all, old man. That's all!"

"Mr. Nicholas, I can't allow you to be excited like this," his nurse protested. "Doctor gave very strict orders—"

"I'm not in the least excited," said Mr. Nicholas. "Stay and make sure, if you like. And you may come in, Hayden, if you can behave like an adult."

"This is private," said Bud, still from the door.

"No. No longer. I tried to keep it so, but that was a mistake—you are no more capable of protecting your sister than I am. This is man's work," said Mr. Nicholas, in the warmth of his anger, "and neither you nor I qualify for it."

Unexpectedly, Bud gave a short laugh. He came in and shut the door—quietly. The nurse's hand moved on Mr. Nicholas's, but she did not speak.

"He's quite a talker, isn't he?" said Bud. He was speaking to her, and his voice was different—the voice of a man at ease with women because he was attractive to them.

"You should be ashamed of yourself," she said.

"Yeah. That's what they tell me."

"No, I mean it. Mr. Nicholas, if you must see this man, I really think you had better wait until—"

"No. This will be very brief. I would rather be finished with it," he said. He turned his face to where Bud now stood, at the foot of his bed. "There is no reason why I shouldn't tell you what I intend to tell the police. Your sister was attacked—nearly violated and murdered, in my empty house. The night before last. I interrupted the attack by accident, and the man got away. She knows who he is. And she is more afraid of telling you what happened than of anything else he may do to her."

There was total silence in the room.

The nurse whispered, "Oh, dear . . ." under her breath, and moved toward the door. "Please don't stay long," she murmured, passing Bud. He didn't reply.

When they were alone he came round the bed and stood over Mr. Nicholas.

"Tell me what happened. Tell me what happened to her."

"I've told you what matters. This man lured her into my house by breaking a window lock and telling her that it was broken. Like any normally adventurous child, she went in to explore. He either entered after her or was lying there in wait. She managed to escape from him, and he locked her in my attic—I suppose she had run there to get away from him. That was where I found her. She was simply crouching there by the door, waiting to fight another hopeless battle with him whenever he should come back. She even hid from me."

"Oh, God," said Bud. "Why didn't she . . ."

He was as tense for her as if it were still happening. But he couldn't think what it was she should have done.

"Why didn't she break a window and call for help? I suggested that—after he came back and locked us in again. But he knew her better than I did. He knew she belonged to a family that makes a profession of being at odds with the world—to whom the police are enemies. The neighbors are enemies. And enemies that she has to fight alone, so that her brother won't get fed up and leave."

"You said he came back."

"He came back twice. In between, he went down and broke the streetlight outside. He had a healthy respect for her, you see—he didn't want her to be able to see at all when he came into that attic."

"Wait a minute," said Bud.

But he did nothing in the pause, neither moved nor spoke. He seemed hardly to breathe.

"You had better sit down," said Mr. Nicholas.

"God damn it, I know what I better do!" he broke out savagely. Then: "No. No. I don't mean that. Go on. Tell me."

"He came in, of course. And we were no match for him. But while he was dealing with me—he hadn't known I was there—Mary Rose was able to escape. She made a lot of noise," said Mr. Nicholas, "so that the man would leave me and follow her. As he did. She came back later and told me he was hiding in an abandoned car in your yard."

"She came *back?*"

"Yes. You weren't home, and she says the back door doesn't lock. Apparently she didn't feel her father was any protection—she was afraid this man would beat him up, too, if he came into your house looking for her. So she came back to my house. There was nowhere else she dared to go. She came back and barricaded us in to wait

A Friend of Mary Rose

for daylight, even though she thought at first that I was dead. That frightened her."

"All right," said Bud. Stopping it. He turned and walked away, to some distant part of the room.

"I've got to get her away. Now. Right now."

"Have you someplace to take her?"

"I'll keep her with me. Every minute. She'll never go near that place again without I'm right there with her. Never."

Mr. Nicholas accepted this for what it was—an outburst of horror, and grief. He didn't comment.

"By God, she'll never go back," Bud said then. "I'll sell that pile of junk—I'll make the old man sell it, even if he has to give it away! Or else he can sit there alone in it and rot in his drink. . . . I'll get a trailer," he said rapidly. "We'll get the hell out of here, I can make good money any place. She'll live in a decent, clean trailer, in a nice place. A new place. She'll go to a new school, and she won't have anything to be ashamed of! And she'll dress like the other girls. Better. She wants to be Mary Rose," he said, "that's what she'll be. From now on."

He came back beside the bed. Mr. Nicholas felt his inspection.

"You put up a fight for her, didn't you?" he said.

"I'm far past the days of being able to do that. She does her own fighting. She has to."

"No, she wouldn't have got away, if you hadn't of been there. I owe you that."

It was an aggressive statement, and Mr. Nicholas was irritated by it.

137

"You owe me nothing. If your sister had any debt to me, she paid it herself."

The consideration of him went on, above him there. Finally Bud said: "Those things you said about her, before. You meant that, didn't you?"

"I meant it. I also meant what I said about reporting this man to the police." In spite of himself, an urgency came into his voice. "He's broken out of control, Bud. He isn't safe to be at large. He'll do it again. If not to Mary Rose, then to some other child."

"Not when I get through with him."

"Oh, yes. Unless you mean to kill him, of course. That would certainly solve all your problems."

"I got no quarrel with you, Mr. Nicholas," Bud said suddenly. "Just don't needle me. . . Look, I'm going home and get the kid now. I got a friend she can stay with for a while. A woman. She'll be okay there, till I can get things straightened out—and I will. But don't you—"

"Is this Lou?" Mr. Nicholas inquired.

Bud drew a long breath.

"You two really had quite a session, didn't you?" he said.

"We had a lot of time. And Mary Rose has a great deal on her mind."

"Yeah," said Bud. "I can see that. All right—I get your message, Mr. Nicholas. It's time Mi—my sister and I talked things over, and we will. But—"

"Privately, I hope. And before you rush into anything."

"Look, I said I got your message. I got it. Now try and get mine," he said earnestly. "You call the cops on this,

A Friend of Mary Rose

and the kid's going to get it just as hard as this guy. If it's Miller, or some bastard like that, his word's as good as hers. Maybe better. Sure you were there," he said, as Mr. Nicholas opened his mouth. "So who was it? Whoever she says? Don't kid yourself, Mr. Nicholas—we don't have that kind of reputation. And what was she doing there, anyway—maybe she went in with him, herself, and then he got a little too rough for her. How about that?"

"Bud—"

"You want to hear this from me, or from them?" he said savagely. "Wake up, Mr. Nicholas—you're a nice old guy, but you got a different orbit, that's all."

"The man will be marked, too," said Mr. Nicholas rapidly.

"You're damn right he'll be marked. . . . So suppose it all goes like the book says," Bud said, quieting. "They believe her. They take in the guy. What happens to him? You think they're going to lock him up for life? Brand him? I'll tell you what happens—he gets about six months for assault, and he goes on the books to watch. Along with about a million other queers. You think they can watch 'em all? So he does his six, he comes out, he moves. And he's back in business. And meanwhile my sister's on the books, too, for being in an empty house at night with a dirty man. That she says she didn't know was there."

"You know she didn't."

"Sure I know. So do you. And if you're the kid's friend, like you say, you'll keep it that way—between the two of us that do believe her. Once you start talking, you're going to find out I'm right. Only that'll be too late."

Mr. Nicholas said thoughtfully, "Bud, I know you believe everything that you're saying. But what if it simply isn't so? If there's another side to this, won't you at least listen to it?"

"Sure. Like what?"

"I don't know. But I intend to find out. Exactly what the procedures and penalties are, for what this man has done. And what protection is available to your sister."

"You want to talk to your lawyer, right?"

"Yes. Without mentioning names."

"Well, you do that," said Bud. "And if he tells you any different than I tell you, you let me know."

"Also, there's a strong possibility that this man may be mentally unbalanced. And able to conceal it only if he's not challenged. If that's the case, he must be found at all costs."

Above him, Bud gave a checked sigh.

"Mister, how can you live so long and be so innocent?" he said, almost kindly. "Sure he's a nut, there's no maybe about it. If you want the God's truth, my old man's another. The street's full of 'em. The world's full of 'em! Once they start rounding up the nuts, where do you think they're going to put 'em all?"

Mr. Nicholas lost patience.

"Don't be absurd—there's a great deal of difference between what you call a 'nut' and a dangerous criminal lunatic! You're the one who's being naïve! A man who would trap a little girl in a deserted house, with the intention of violating her—undoubtedly of murdering her—"

A Friend of Mary Rose

"Now stop right there," said Bud. "How much of that can you prove? No—hold it. Think it over. This guy didn't kill anybody. He didn't rape anybody. He—"

"Do you mean to wait until he does?"

Bud's urgent voice became more remote. He had straightened up.

"Not me," he said. "I'm not patient, like the legal beagles, Mr. Nicholas. I know what was in his dirty black heart as well as you do. As well as he does. And I know what to do about it. There's no red tape round my hands. And no headshrinker telling me what to do. I can get through to him just fine—the way he'll remember every time he looks at another kid, his whole dirty life. And strictly private, Mr. Nicholas. He'll take what he takes and keep shut about it, don't worry about that."

"Why?" Mr. Nicholas demanded. "If he has as little to fear as you say?"

Bud gave his short laugh.

"You should be a lawyer yourself," he said, without rancor. "All right, call your guy—take your time, talk it over. That's the bargain, right? You don't blow any whistles, I don't make any move. And then we'll see who's right."

He was moving toward the door. Mr. Nicholas said urgently, "But when will I see you again? Are you coming back?"

"Sure, I'll drop by—or I'll give you a ring. I'll be in touch with you, don't worry, Mr. Nicholas. And don't worry about my sister any more. I mean it. Maybe it's a rotten thing to say, but I guess we needed something to happen to us—thank God it wasn't worse. So don't worry about her—she's going to be all right from now on, believe me."

"She won't be all right unless you are, Bud," said Mr. Nicholas. He called it out, despairingly, to the closing door; but either Bud did not hear or he did not want to talk any more. The door shut quietly, finally, and his rapid steps went off down the hall. They were the steps of a man impatient to be on his way, with a lot to do. And no intentions of coming back again.

Chapter Twelve

Whatever Bud's intentions had been, something changed them. He came back the next morning.

To Mr. Nicholas, he seemed almost a different person—much quieter, much less hostile. Almost diffident in his need to talk things over with someone he could trust. He was, in fact, the young man Mr. Nicholas had tried to find the day before—and now here he was, a day too late.

For something had happened to Mr. Nicholas, too. It was not exactly discouragement. Perhaps it was partly cumulative fatigue—and no doubt all those bedpans were beginning to tell on his spirit. Mostly, though, he was just homesick.

Dorothea and his grandchildren had come to visit him the afternoon before; and while the visit had gone very well, even cheerfully, he had not felt homesick then. Not even when they told him about his cat, who missed him and cried in the night, shut into his room alone (apparently Dorothea had known about this all along). Nor about his trunks, which she had finally decided to keep right in his new room, no matter how it looked. And all the details of the new house, and the new neighborhood—he had enjoyed these, but felt no particular haste to confirm them. But that night, he had dreamed that he was home. Home was not the old house—it was not, in fact, any particular place. So far as he could puzzle it out after he woke, it was just a long awareness of being where he belonged: of hearing Dorothea's coming and going, her occasional voice, her footsteps and perfectly definable activities. That was the whole dream; it seemed to go on a long time, and it absorbed him completely. When he woke and knew that it had been a dream, he felt quite lost, and rather humiliated. Why, that was no better than a big baby, content simply to lie all day listening to its mother! Had he really sunk to such a state? He knew, of course, that he had not—and yet the memory of the dream clung, nostalgic and shameful, long after he had repudiated it.

The dream had also cut him off from Mary Rose. She lay somewhere on the other side of it, as if in a far past—a puzzling and pitiful little girl whom he had not been able to help. Someone else's little girl, though, and not really his concern at all.

He thought, I'm being old this morning, that's what it is. This is what old age is like. I suppose it's time. . . . But it depressed him; he did not like to be so good.

Nor did he want to cope with Bud again. Even a good Bud. Why was he here? What did he want? He sat politely on the chair beside the bed, smelling of shaving

A Friend of Mary Rose

lotion and car grease, and asked if Mr. Nicholas had talked to his lawyer.

Mr. Nicholas had. He was able to say, without satisfaction, that Bud had been quite wrong about the light sentence. From the way the man had behaved, Mr. Marks thought it more than probable that he would be given extensive tests, and probably sent to a mental institution: the criminal assault would serve as a legal control to get the man where he really belonged, before he qualified for a life sentence—or the electric chair.

Besides, Mr. Marks doubted that the man had got to this stage without some preliminary troubles, or warnings, which should be on record.

"Already on the books, hey?" said Bud thoughtfully. "Well, maybe. Could be."

What Mr. Nicholas did not go into was Joe's insistence on their being able to identify the man absolutely. Mr. Nicholas admitted that from this particular encounter he couldn't do it. But if he was to be confronted with him again, even sober, he felt sure that he could.

"Could, or would?" said Joe shrewdly. "Come on, Nick, you're completely dependent on this girl's word for it, aren't you? And how's she going to stand up for a witness? She ever been in any sex trouble before?"

"Certainly not! And what do you mean, *before?*" added Mr. Nicholas, angrily.

Still, faintly, his anger came back when he thought of it. In the end, Joe's advice had been to report the attack at once, and let the police take over from there. Without any more delay, either. A day or two was allowable, at

145

his age, and being in the hospital. But no more; or else it would begin to look fishy. As if he didn't trust the girl himself, maybe.

"I trust her absolutely," said Mr. Nicholas.

He still did. But he was beginning to have a faint, exhausted resentment at the Haydens in general. They were the hardest people to reach he had ever come across. It would serve them right if he did as Joe suggested, and reported his own attack and the presence of the man and the girl without identifying either. After all, Mary Rose had carefully not told him who she was.

Yet he couldn't bring himself to this deception. Nor could he report her. How could he expect anyone else to understand that she would conceal such an experience? They would think the worst of her. They might even think, as Bud said, that she had gone with the man voluntarily, and then taken fright.

No; he couldn't do it.

He didn't even want to talk about it any more.

Yet here was Bud, troubled and persistent, camped beside his bed. Mr. Nicholas had a good idea what had happened: Mary Rose wouldn't tell him who the man was, either. He lay and waited for Bud to confess this, so he could tell him it served him right.

But Bud was taking the long way round.

"I admit I can't see Pop in the trailer," he was saying. "And I can understand how she don't want to go anywheres without him. But it's crazy to think we can fix that place up and live there different, with him like he is. No woman's going to put up with him, even if I could

A Friend of Mary Rose

afford to hire somebody. Or even if I got married. . . ."

Mr. Nicholas made no comment.

"Well, it's not your worry," said Bud, accepting this. "It's just that yesterday you—I guess you made pretty good sense, and it's the first time I ever talked about it with anybody. I mean, that didn't have some crazy ax to grind."

"I had an ax to grind," Mr. Nicholas said grimly.

Bud laughed.

"Yeah. You sure are for that kid, aren't you?"

But Mr. Nicholas wasn't falling into this trap again. He said nothing.

"Well, so am I," said Bud. "But what the hell am I going to do with her? She can't handle Pop, and he can't handle her—and I can't handle the both of them! Brother, if he knew what happened this time, she'd really get it."

Against his better judgment, Mr. Nicholas said: "You haven't told your father about this?"

"Jeez, no—he'd blow the roof off!"

"Do you mean he would beat her? For being attacked and beaten?"

Startled, Bud said: "No—he wouldn't do that—"

There was a long silence, and then Bud got up.

"Maybe you got something there, Mr. Nicholas," he said. "Okay. Thanks. I'll see you."

Mr. Nicholas had never heard of a family so completely out of touch with itself and the world around it. He was thoroughly out of patience with them. All of them.

He was out of patience with everybody.

Dr. Linen came by and approved of his gloom. He said, "You're letting down nicely. Now you can see just how much that business took out of you."

"Is that what you intended?"

"Well, there's no way round it. Unless you keep on going till you drop. Like me," he said cheerfully.

Mr. Nicholas lay silently hating him till he went away.

His family came that evening and found him totally unresponsive. If he had spoken at all, he would have been particularly disagreeable to Dorothea, and he wasn't going to give her that much satisfaction. As it was, she kept a hurt silence, and Johnny did the talking.

He said he had gone by Mrs. Thompson's and taken her a Spring Assortment. She was feeling lonely and rather dull, after all the excitement, and John had taken it on himself to offer to bring her over for the day as soon as they got settled. Was that all right? Mr. Nicholas supposed it was. Then John produced the queer little note someone had left at Mrs. Thompson's house, the morning his father had been there, and read it out.

"What do you think of that, Dad?" he said. "There must have been some kid peeking in at you—and you must have lost consciousness for quite a while, you know. Did you realize it?"

"Let me have the note," said his father.

It was crumpled and much folded by now, and he could feel nothing except periods, and perhaps a crossbar. But his fingers went over and over it, in some idiot hope of their own. From which they got nothing, of course. It

A Friend of Mary Rose

didn't even have any smell, except Johnny's tobacco.

That night he got only a pill to sleep on, and it didn't carry him through. In some still premorning hour he had another attack of panic for Mary Rose—not quite so severe, but entirely sobering. In the morning, as soon as he could hope for an answer, he called Al's Service Station.

Bud wasn't there, somebody told him, but they would tell him to call Mr. Nicholas when he came in. Time passed; he didn't call. Mr. Nicholas decided that he would come by instead, in his lunch hour. By two o'clock he conceded to himself that the lunch hour was past, and called the service station again. At that point, he began to wonder what he had to say.

In fact, he had only to say his name, and Bud's voice warmed into loquacity.

"Gee, I wanted to get over and see you, Mr. Nicholas," he began. "But I already took so much time off yesterday, I got kind of behind here. But you really started something with us! I told my old man about the kid, like you said, and you know what he did?"

"What?"

"He sent for the priest! How do you like that? All these years he won't let him in the door, and last night I had to go over after him. Boy, I was scared to go."

"The priest?" It would never have occurred to Mr. Nicholas, an active Episcopalian, to send for his own priest at such a time. He said with interest: "Why, Bud?"

"Who knows? Anyway, he's really in for it now. The kid isn't even confirmed, the old man hasn't been to confession in ten years—me, too—it's a mess! And I was bringing the kid over here with me after school, you know? She could sit in the office here, and do her homework, and talk to the guys—she wanted to. But no more. Now I got to take her over, she stays with the Father's housekeeper till I can pick her up, she works on her catechism—brother, I'm telling you, it's one mess!"

But he sounded cheerful about it.

Mr. Nicholas said urgently, "But that man, Bud—hasn't she said yet who he is?"

Bud's voice altered. He said, "Well, you know, I think you might have been wrong about that, Mr. Nicholas. That was another thing I wanted to ask you about. What made you so sure she knew him, and all? It's more like she really didn't, you know? Like she says, it was pretty dark in there, and everything happened so fast, when he showed . . . What made you feel like she knew him?" he asked again.

Mr. Nicholas opened his mouth, and closed it. His first exasperation went down almost unrecognized. Caution settled on him, like a calmness.

"Well, I did have that impression, Bud," he said.

"Yeah, I know—but why? From the way it sounds, it was more like some bum that was holed up there for the night. I guess she was pretty scared when you were talking to her—but if you could have heard her last night, I think you—"

"As a matter of fact, I would like to see her again," Mr. Nicholas said, adding cunning to caution. "It would give me a great deal of pleasure to talk to her in ordinary circumstances, you know. It's difficult to efface the impression of her as a child in trouble."

This piece of diplomatic pleading went down very well. Bud said thoughtfully, "Yeah, I see what you mean. I guess I should have thought of bringing her over, but everything's been happening so fast—"

"Why don't you bring her to me after school today?" Mr. Nicholas suggested. "And leave her here till you want to pick her up? I'm sure we can find plenty to do, and she could have something to eat here with me."

"Well, thanks—maybe I could check with you later?" Bud sounded embarrassed. "See, I don't want to upset the old man's applecart, you know it really hit him, how she didn't dare stay in the house because I wasn't there. He's thrown out the bottles, he's cleaning the joint up, I got to clean up the yard, and so on. How long it's going to last I wouldn't know, but right now it's like he's got all these plans, him and the Father, and I wouldn't want to mess them up. Maybe I could call you?"

"If you will. I hope very much you can bring her, Bud," said Mr. Nicholas.

It was an understatement.

Around four o'clock Bud called again, still embarrassed. He had just dropped his sister at the priest's, but he was going to bring her by the hospital that evening for a visit, if that was okay? They wouldn't stay very long, but she wanted to see him—only she thought she had better stick to the new plan about afternoons. Was that okay?

Mr. Nicholas "got the message." She wanted to have

her brother with her when they talked. She didn't want to upset any applecarts either. The past was past; no one but dogged old "Mr. Nicklis" threatened her new life, and she didn't want any interference from him. He said grimly that this was quite all right, and settled to wait—without pleasure—for an encounter that would be false, and brief, and useless.

Yet for the second time, she took him by surprise. Her pleasure at seeing him again was real—he couldn't doubt it. In the quiet bustle of the evening visiting hour she came into his room almost running (in some light, hard-soled slippers) and then stopped dead at the bed's edge, without sending one tremor through it. He was sitting up; and to the hand he automatically raised—half in defense, half to see with—she eagerly touched her own. He enclosed it at once; it was Mary Rose's hand.

She said delightedly: "You know it's me, don't you? Even if you didn't know I was coming, you could tell—couldn't you, Mr. Nicholas?"

She was turned away, wanting her brother to hear, and to acknowledge her friend's accomplishments.

Her brother said, "Kid, the whole world knows it's you. Now simmer down, you're not supposed to run in hospitals."

"It's all right," said Mr. Nicholas hastily. "How are you, child? How are you?"

He was astonished by his own happiness—as instant as it was unexpected. As if he had told Bud the truth without realizing it: that all he wanted was to encounter the real Mary Rose, really freed from her fears and dangers.

For that moment, he was as willing to forget as she.

Evidently, she was nicely dressed, and wanted him to notice—or wanted to show Bud that he *could* notice—for she guided his hand to her chest.

"It's my new dress," she explained. "It's purple—my father bought it! He went with Mrs. Reilly, she used to take care of me when I was little, and she might come and housekeep for us if he gets a job. . . ." Her voice grew absent; she said suddenly: "It's the first time I saw you so good, Mr. Nicholas. Do you want to see me?"

"Yes," he said, not understanding or caring much what she meant, absorbed in her lively nearness. "Yes, I should like that."

She sat carefully on the edge of his bed and put his hand against her cheek, and left it there. After a moment he understood, and not to disappoint her, made a careful exploration of the small face. He was not expert at this, and did not learn much, except that her rough hair had been carefully smoothed.

"Why," he said gravely, "you have blue eyes!"

She drew in her breath so sharply that he added at once: "I'm only teasing, child."

"But it's true!"

"Guessing, then. Bud, look on my dresser—are there cookies?" There were, and bottles of Coke—he had asked for them out of a sense of duty, but he was glad now that they were there.

And he did not disturb their brief party by any warnings, or references, that would make Mary Rose withdraw. But as it became clear that the Haydens were not going to leave their neighborhood but were, on the contrary, going to pull themselves together and face it down—Millers and all—a grave intention began to grow in him.

Mary Rose could not build her new life on this pact of secrecy with a vicious, dangerous man. Nor could Mr. Nicholas—yet—persuade her of this. Especially not with Joe Marks's skepticism still in his own mind, about the child's reliability as a witness. *But if Mr. Nicholas himself could identify the man*—independently—then there could be no more reason for keeping quiet. He would have no more hesitation in openly urging Mary Rose and her family—and her priest, if necessary—to start their new life as they meant to go on. Openly, and lawfully.

Only how could he manage it?

Mr. Nicholas grew so thoughtful that Bud took his sister away, afraid she had exhausted the old man. She went obediently, but left him a present—a small box filled with things which, she said, were nice to feel. Some of them he could—absently exploring—identify without trouble: stones and marbles, stripped and smoothed twigs of odd design. Others, such as a piece of new chamois, took him longer. But there was a plastic or celluloid shape he could make nothing of; and during the long night he returned gratefully to this puzzle, when he needed rest from the graver problem weighing on his mind.

Chapter Thirteen

By morning he had his plan, and felt that he was ready to put it into action.

Dr. Linen, perhaps in remorse, had taken him off the bedpan the day before, and by now he was navigating pretty freely. His legs were fine. His head was fine. He didn't even mind the harness round his middle. He could, in fact, have gone home—the doctor himself agreed with this.

But Mr. Nicholas didn't want to go home. What he desired—and proposed—was that he should be a kind of latchkey patient for another day or so, with the privilege of spending his evenings in Rudds' Grocery Store, staying until they closed. Then he would taxi back to the hospital and go to bed. Since this was Friday, he had every hope that one or two evenings of listening would suffice. Rudds' was the only local source of beer in the evenings, and their weekend trade must comprise the whole neighborhood, surely.

Dr. Linen wanted to know what he meant to do if he

did identify his attacker—trip him up with his stick and then step on him? Mr. Nicholas replied seriously that he meant to ask the Rudds, now and then, who some customer had been, and in this way obscure the real information he wanted. When he had it, he would simply leave—after an interval.

"And what's the fellow going to think, if he comes in and sees you sitting there?" Dr. Linen demanded. "Don't you think he'll guess what you're up to?"

"I hope so," said Mr. Nicholas. "There isn't much he can do about it. He certainly won't risk attacking me in a public place. Of course he might see me and not come in, but I'll try not to be visible from the outside. And I'll know him this time, Roger—no matter how he tries to walk or speak, I'll know him."

Dr. Linen then pointed out that the hospital was not a hotel, and that he certainly could not go out for the evening and come rolling in at midnight. Of course, if he thought Dorothea wouldn't mind his having a little night life, Dr. Linen had no objection to his going home.

Mr. Nicholas now perceived that his earnest plan was making no impression—that his friend was worse than skeptical, he was amused.

He said, "I think I had better tell you why the identification of this man is so important, Roger"; and then, much as he had told it to Bud, he repeated the story of their encounter in the empty house. He added to this what he had learned of Mary Rose and her circumstances. And finally, he explained the necessity for a positive identification, as Joe Marks had explained it to him. Dr. Linen listened without interrupting, as he did to interesting symptoms.

At the end, he said only: "Well, I agree with your friend Marks, that you ought to turn the whole mess over to the police and bow out. But if you're going to adopt little wild girls at your age, I suppose I can't expect rational behavior."

His manner was different, though. He was serious now.

Mr. Nicholas said, "Perhaps Lettie Thompson would put me up again for a night or two."

"You keep away from that poor woman, she's had enough of you. No," said his friend decisively, "if you're set on this business, you'd better come to us. Then I can keep an eye on you. And my wife's used to characters, she'll see that you behave."

Mr. Nicholas said that was very kind, and would be considerably easier to explain to Dorothea than another visit to Lettie.

"And I want to take you there and pick you up," Dr. Linen added. "You're not to set foot out of the place without me, do you hear? Actually, someone ought to wait with you—Johnny, perhaps. I don't like you sitting there alone so long."

"It won't be long, I'm only interested in the evening hours, and they close at eleven." Mr. Nicholas, relieved to find his friend being drawn in, went on: "Besides, the Rudds are always there, one or both of them, I'm sure. And an able-bodied person sitting there with me would be much too obvious. No one minds an old blind man sitting around, he's quite anonymous," he said impersonally.

Dr. Linen was taken aback by this self-description—which he wouldn't have used, himself, of his friend, and didn't much like to hear Mr. Nicholas using.

He said, "Well, get some rest, and I'll pick you up later today. Since you're bound to do this." And went away in a state of indecision not usual to him.

Explaining their proposed visitor to his wife, he said: "I don't suppose it'll hurt the old fellow to sit there playing detective for an evening or two. It'll relieve his mind, anyway—he'll have done what he could, about a very nasty business. Though I wouldn't want to spend that long with the Rudds myself," he added. "But that's his problem." And having in this way made up his mind, he began to be amused again at the idea of this unlikely company, and curious to see how Mr. Nicholas would handle it.

Both Rudds were on duty when they arrived, at a little after seven that evening. Mild weather, and the beginning of the weekend, had brought DeKuyper Street largely out of doors; and its corner store was still doing a brisk "supper" business. Mrs. Rudd, behind the counter, noticed them first. Her expression altered, to a different intentness, and she came out to them.

"Well, good evening, doctor—and here's Mr. Nicholas, looking just as spry as ever, isn't he? My, you certainly gave us all a shock, that day you went off in the ambulance—first the moving vans and then the ambulance, I

A Friend of Mary Rose

thought my goodness, I bet Mrs. Nicholas doesn't know which way she's going. A fall, was it?"

"A slight accident. Thank you. Very nice of you to be concerned," said Mr. Nicholas. "And now I wonder if I might trespass on your kindness, Mrs. Rudd."

"You want some bananas," she said, with a quick glance at the doctor. "I'll get them for you right now. About how many?"

"No, as a matter of fact, I don't require anything. But I should like very much to wait in some corner here, if I may, for a while."

"Wait here?" Mrs. Rudd glanced at the doctor again, who was looking idly round, nodding to an occasional patient. "You're waiting for someone?"

"Yes," he said. "I should appreciate being able to wait here."

"Oh." Her glance went to the back of the store, to where her husband had been when they arrived—a broad back at the big refrigerator. But he was no longer in sight. She made up her mind alone, and quickly. "Why, surely," she said, with her anguished smile. "No matter how busy we are, I guess we can still do a favor for an old neighbor, isn't that right, doctor? After all, we're not one of those supermarkets that don't even know who their neighbors are, not that Mrs. Nicholas doesn't have the right to shop anywhere she wants, that's what a democracy's for. But I wouldn't want anything else to happen to you, it gets so crowded in here sometimes—we wouldn't want that, would we, doctor?"

"Nothing will happen to me, Mrs. Rudd," Mr. Nicholas

said patiently. "Thank you. I wonder if I might use the chair you used to keep here? Perhaps you would ask Mr. Rudd."

"The chair?" she repeated. There was a small pause; then she said tightly, "Just a minute," and left them.

Dr. Linen watched her go into the back premises, past the three or four remaining customers—a small bustling woman in search of something she wasn't going to find. Rudd, a pale-eyed, heavy blond man, given to striped shirts under his soiled butcher's apron, was popularly supposed to be henpecked; but Dr. Linen did not agree. He preferred to consider him a potential wife-beater, whom Mrs. Rudd could not rouse to his duties.

She reappeared alone, her pale face pinched with annoyance, and began to wait on the nearest customer without another glance at the two men by the door. Dr. Linen murmured, "I don't think your plan is going to get off the ground, my friend." To which Mr. Nicholas replied quietly: "Why don't you go, Roger? I'm all right."

"I want to see what happens when she finds out how long you mean to wait."

But less patient than his friend, he presently walked over to the counter.

"If your husband's busy, perhaps I can get the chair, Mrs. Rudd," he said briskly. "Mr. Nicholas ought not to stand long."

She looked up at him then—with such open longing to quarrel that he felt some sympathy for her. But her control was remarkable. She managed another of those aching smiles.

"He's gone to deliver. We're very busy."

"I see you are. You'd better let me help."

Without a word, she turned and went into the back premises—returned past the curtain, awkwardly bearing the chair herself. It was an old wooden straight chair which had stood in one corner for years, certainly no invitation to loll, and usually covered with boxes. But she said in a rush of sweetness, handing it over: "People hang around so if they can sit down—I had to put it in back. But you're welcome to use it, doctor."

Remarkable control. He thanked her gravely, and then looked round for a place to put Mr. Nicholas, who was still standing patiently by the door. He found a niche behind the bread stand, from which his friend could not be seen from the street, and placed the chair there. Then he guided Mr. Nicholas to it.

Seated, Mr. Nicholas said in a low voice, "Thank you, Roger. I hadn't expected so much difficulty—Mrs. Rudd always seemed excessively pleasant, the few mornings I came down. Do you think something is wrong?"

"No more than usual," Dr. Linen said, grinning. "Sure you want to stay?"

Mr. Nicholas hesitated and then said: "I think I must. But you go along. And thank you."

"Call me if you change your mind. And remember—stay put."

Mr. Nicholas said he would, and the doctor left—wondering how long his friend would stick it out.

Mr. Nicholas himself had no such wonder—he meant to stay until closing, unless he were actually put out, which seemed unlikely. But he hadn't foreseen the obstacle of being unwelcome, added to the general unpleasantness of his task.

For he did not want to do this. Dr. Linen's idea of him as "playing detective" was far from true. He dreaded these lonely, public hours of listening for the entrance of a man whom he abhorred more than he had realized. His dread was not physical—certainly no second beating was going to take place in this open, lighted store. Only an encounter lay ahead, if he was lucky. A second encounter, when the man would see him sitting there and in that moment of surprise—he hoped—would betray himself in his breathing, his movements, his whole manner. That was all that could happen; Mr. Nicholas did not know why he dreaded it so. And afterward, he had only to inquire who that man had been.

But he would have to inquire of Mrs. Rudd. A hostile Mrs. Rudd, who perhaps would not even bother to answer? He considered this, anxiously, and tried to gauge her temper from her voice. There was no doubt that it changed, whenever it came in his direction. She did resent his being there.

Why? Did she have some grudge against his family that he did not know about? Did she dislike him personally? Or did she simply feel that her property was being encroached upon, without profit to her? Mr. Nicholas began to realize that his supposed familiarity with the Rudds was one of hearsay, rather than experience. They were emergency suppliers for Dorothea, who would send one of the children down to the corner for something she had run out of; and his knowledge of them was based almost entirely on this long, reluctant patronage of hers. He wasn't pleased to find a part of his mind stocked with Dorothea's opinions disguised as his own; but since he had no others, he attempted to sort these out. His impression was that Dorothea preferred to deal with Mr. Rudd, who was less tense than his wife, and that Rudd usually took the evening hours in the store. Certainly Mr. Nicholas had never encountered him there on one of his morning visits. So probably the wife opened the store, and the husband closed it, and if this was true Mr. Nicholas might hope that Rudd would soon relieve Mrs. Rudd, and prove less hostile. He could hardly be more so.

A pause came, in which there were no customers in the store, and Mr. Nicholas was not surprised when Mrs. Rudd came over to question him.

"Well, you're having a long wait, aren't you?" she said (although he had not been there half an hour). "Don't you think I'd better call up and find out what's the matter? I'm sure Mrs. Nicholas wouldn't want you to be sitting around this way, with every nosy person on the block asking about her business—now would she?"

It was true that several persons had stopped briefly to speak to him, rather to his surprise. On the porch, probably, he had been too far for casual conversations. But he did not like this interpretation of their neighborliness.

"I'm competent to deal with nosiness, Mrs. Rudd," he replied. "If there should be any. You have very pleasant customers," he added. "You're fortunate in them."

"Well," she said, distracted, "of course we've been here

a long while. People know us. And we don't encourage the riffraff—that cheap candy business, I had to get rid of that. It just wasn't worth it, for what it brought in."

"I suppose not."

"Well," she said, returning to business, "I don't like to hurry an old—an old neighbor, but I don't want to go upstairs and leave you here, Mr. Nicholas. I just don't feel your daughter-in-law would want me to do that, especially after all the trouble she's had already. Why don't you let me call up and see what's the matter? Is it your son you're waiting for?"

"No, my son isn't coming for me tonight," he replied. "Dr. Linen will pick me up again when you close, if the person I'm waiting for shouldn't appear. You needn't worry about my being left on your hands."

"When we close!" she repeated. "Well, that's quite a time, I mean that's quite a responsibility, Mr. Nicholas! We always like to be as obliging as we can, but after all, we're busy people! This is a business, and that's a long time to have to be responsible for someone's—for someone. I just think you'd better go wait somewhere else, Mr. Nicholas!"

That controlled waspishness was escaping at last, with no Dr. Linen to appreciate it.

Mr. Nicholas said, without expression, "I'm afraid there is nowhere else to wait for this person. I have no other way of reaching him. Privately, that is."

"Well, I don't know what you mean by *that*," she exclaimed, in a luxury of release. "*'Privately'* isn't exactly

A Friend of Mary Rose

what I'd call a busy store, where hard-working people are trying to earn a *living—!*"

"Myra . . ."

This one low sound, from the back of the store, startled them both. It silenced Mrs. Rudd, but only momentarily. In the next moment, she had turned and started rapidly toward the speaker.

"Where have you been?" she demanded, in a new, more fretful voice. "Do you realize I've been alone here nearly an hour? And you didn't even take the beer down to . . . and leaving me with . . . sit there all *night* . . ."

She was behind the curtain that partitioned the back premises from the store, and had lowered her voice, but not much. Her husband's lower voice obscured whatever words he was offering in reply. They were not many.

Whatever they were, his wife received them indignantly. Mr. Nicholas, a helpless audience, heard her say: ". . . think I'm made of! You didn't even . . ." He interrupted, his words still obscure, and she broke in upon him—and then a customer came into the store.

It was a man, absently whistling. Tapping with his nails on the counter, while he waited. His brief inspection of silent Mr. Nicholas didn't reconcile him to waiting.

"Hey!" he called out. "Anybody home?"

Mrs. Rudd's rapid footsteps went up some stairs; and presently, a slower bass accompaniment, her husband's steps came into the front of the store.

He said nothing, not even to the impatient man's "Six Piel's—you got it cold?" For answer, the heavy refriger-

Elizabeth Fenwick

ator door opened and shut, and then the cash register. The impatient man went out, still whistling, and the door shut behind him.

Mr. Nicholas, raising his head, said: "Good evening, Mr. Rudd."

Rudd shifted his feet, there behind the counter. He muttered finally, "Don't mind about her. It's her nerves. She's a very nervous woman. Afterwards, she's sorry."

"She has no need to be sorry, so far as I'm concerned," Mr. Nicholas replied.

The feet moved again.

"You can sit here if you want," said Rudd's voice.

"Thank you."

"It don't bother me."

Mr. Nicholas said nothing to this; and after a moment the refrigerator door opened again.

"You want a beer?"

Mr. Nicholas declined. He heard the rush of escaping gas as a beer can was punctured, and then two women came into the store, talking together. This time Mr. Rudd greeted them: "Good evening, ladies," and the three of them talked while the women's purchases were collected and paid for. When they had gone, the silence returned. Rudd broke it.

"It even makes her nervous if I take a beer in the store," he said, a man continuing conversation. "So—what can you do? I wait till she goes up."

He laughed, and drank. Mr. Nicholas's continuing quiet seemed to encourage him.

"A nervous woman you can't argue with. You know?

A Friend of Mary Rose

You can't even talk to a nervous woman, it just makes her nervous."

Another customer entered while he was speaking, and two more while the first was still there. When all three finally were gone, another beer can was punctured.

"So you just want to sit here and wait awhile, that's right?" said Rudd, when he had drunk. "Till the doctor comes back for you?"

"That's right."

"Well, why not? It don't bother anybody. You can sit here, I don't care." His first constraint was gone; he sounded at ease now, even slightly contemptuous. Mr. Nicholas faced across the room toward him.

"Will you come and help me up, Mr. Rudd?" he said then.

"You want to get up?"

"Please."

With interest—and without moving—Rudd said: "You can't get up by yourself since you got hurt?"

"I'll be glad of your help."

"Sure, all right."

But he still did not move.

"What happened to you, anyway? I heard you went in the ambulance."

"Nothing of any consequence."

Neither of them spoke, until Rudd spoke again.

"Maybe you better stay there like the doc put you," he said. "Maybe that's better."

"Nonsense," said Mr. Nicholas. "There's no reason

why I shouldn't get up. Is there any reason why you shouldn't help me to?"

"Sure, I'll help you," said Rudd again. But his feet, coming into sluggish motion, went toward the refrigerator. "You don't want a beer?"

Mr. Nicholas didn't answer. The heavy door opened and shut again, the can was punctured. Rudd drank. No one came in.

Then the can was set down, the slow steps came round the counter and down the middle of the floor. Within several feet of Mr. Nicholas they stopped again.

"What did you want to get up for?" he asked.

"I want to use your telephone, if I may."

"Sure, I'll call for you," said Rudd. "Who do you want to call up?"

"Thank you, but I had better make this call myself," said Mr. Nicholas. As he spoke he reached out his hand, saying firmly: "Just take my hand, please."

He had his stick braced and ready, in his other hand, and kept his posture of readiness until, after a pause, Rudd shuffled forward. An experimental hand touched his. He took it at once, checking its movement of withdrawal, and at the same time forced himself quickly up.

"There, you see?" he said. "Quite simple."

As he said this, dropping the supporting hand, he seemed in some overconfidence to lose balance, and his hand flew up again—far up, touching and then grasping the other's hair. Only for a moment; before Rudd could strike out, cursing, at the grasping hand, Mr. Nicholas had withdrawn it.

"Clumsy of me . . ."

Leaning on his stick, a little out of breath, he heard Rudd blunder away, out of reach, and stand with his own harder breathing filling the little store's silence.

"You startle easily, Mr. Rudd," said Mr. Nicholas. "You have caught some of your wife's nervousness."

Like an evoked nightmare, the familiar thick whispering broke out: "You devil! You old devil . . ."

It stopped, abruptly. There were several fast, heavy steps, and then the sound of the front door being slammed and locked. And then the blind was pulled down.

Chapter Fourteen

Mr. Nicholas said quietly, "What is the point of that? I am known to be here. You had better not make your position any worse."

Rudd, breathing, went on drawing down blinds—one for each large window on either side of the door. When he had done this, some feeling of refuge let him stop. He did nothing but stand waiting—breathing. As if the next move were Mr. Nicholas's.

Who went on: "I suppose you realize that you were lucky, in my house. You did not commit any serious crime, at least not according to the law. Don't spoil your luck now, Mr. Rudd."

He didn't expect an answer at once—not from this slow mind with its wild underlay of alarms. But with hardly any delay, Rudd blurted out: "You come here to make trouble for me—don't do it! I'll make trouble, too—"

"You already have. Be glad it's no worse. Now open that door again, before someone notices it."

Rudd went past him. Widely round him, to the back of the store. The refrigerator door opened and shut again.

Mr. Nicholas briefly debated whether or not to go and open the door himself. Rudd was twice the distance from it now that he was. Rudd was also twice as agile; and above all, Mr. Nicholas knew he must avoid throwing the man into a panic, in which he would use his physical strength without thinking of consequences.

Oddly, Mr. Nicholas felt no fear. That seizure of physical terror in his own bathroom had left no echo in him. In fact, he felt no emotion, now that he was beyond the emotions of wonder and surprise, and had come to certainty. A certainty without anger, without satisfaction or any excitement. Only a grim determination filled him— to finish this, and be done with it forever.

He said deliberately, "I intend to identify you as the man who entered my empty house and attacked me there when I surprised you. Deny it if you like. If you attack me again, here, you will simply prove what I say. And this time, Dr. Linen is my witness."

"I never touched you," Rudd muttered, from his refuge. "I never would have touched you before, but you hit me first! You were up there with that kid—that dirty kid—everybody knows she's a liar—"

"I'm not interested in your story," Mr. Nicholas said coldly. "You had better keep it. Now are you going to open this door, or shall I?"

Rudd didn't move. But he went on talking, with gathering grievance.

"What do you want to believe that dirty kid for?

Everybody on the block knows about her—she got into your house herself, I seen her! I only went in to make her come out, that's all! And I only knocked you down because you jumped me like that, you hit me first! How did I know?"

"I see you have your story prepared," said Mr. Nicholas, with contempt.

"I only went in to make her come out," Rudd repeated doggedly. "On account of her old man—he already had enough bad luck, everybody's sorry for him. Everybody knows what kind of a kid he's got! And then you jumped me like that—how did I know who you were? You better not say I was up there with that kid, because I wasn't—that was you up there, you was the one up there with her! I only went in to make her come out, that's all."

Someone came up and rattled the door, knocked on it.

Mr. Nicholas moved, but Rudd was faster. The beer can dropped clattering to the floor, and he passed Mr. Nicholas like a running bear.

"Closed! Closed!" he bawled against his blinded door. "We got sickness—we're closed!"

Someone spoke inaudibly from the other side—and went away. Immediately, Rudd ran back again to his refuge, and there came the click of a light switch—then another. The smell of his sweating fear hung in the air where he had passed.

"You are making your own story absurd by behaving this way," said Mr. Nicholas. "When Dr. Linen comes back and finds the store closed, he won't go away—I promise you that."

A Friend of Mary Rose

Rudd burst out, almost in a sob: "What do you want to do this for? Why do you want to make all this trouble? I told you—I told you I wouldn't have touched you, only you come at me like that—you and that kid! You was the ones that was up there! I only come in to get her out, and then you both jumped me—"

A door opened, somewhere within the building, and a woman's voice called faintly: "Will! What is it? What's that noise?"

"Nothing—nothing! Go to bed, Myra!"

"But what was that noise?"

She was coming down the stairs. His helpless silence waited to be found.

Her voice became clearer, and sharpened with discovery.

"What have you got the lights out for? Will! *Will!* What are you doing—where are you?"

"Here," he said, hopeless.

He was evidently near her; her voice sank at once.

"What are you doing?"

He mumbled, "That old man—he's trying to make trouble, I had to shut the store—"

She took this in. Then her voice came again, tense and quiet.

"Will, where is he? What did you do?"

"I'm here, Mrs. Rudd," Mr. Nicholas said clearly. "Waiting for your husband to control himself."

Instantly she spat at him: "You get out of here! Get out!"

"Gladly. But your husband has locked me in, for some reason."

She was silent again, perhaps turning to her husband.

His sobbing voice broke out then: "Myra—oh, God, he's got some crazy story, he's going to tell the police—"

"What story? What are you talking about?"

"Oh, God, I don't know—some dirty kid got in his house that night, I only went in to get her out—I didn't know he was there, I wouldn't have touched him, only he—"

"What kid?"

Her fierce demand froze him. He couldn't produce any more coherence, only sobbing breath. There was a sudden scuffle of sound, as if she had seized on him.

"It was that dirty Hayden kid, wasn't it? Wasn't it?"

"Myra—the old man out there, be quiet—"

She was quiet.

There was a muted click—perhaps some other light switch in the back, which would shed a smaller light throughout the store. Mr. Nicholas, halfway to the front door, stopped and turned as her rapid steps came toward him.

She came directly to him and slapped him hard across the face. There was a hoarse cry: *"Myra!"* from the back of the store. She paid no attention to it.

"So you came here to make trouble, did you?" she began in a rapid, low voice. "We're not good enough for you and your stuck-up family—the whole neighborhood's not good enough for you! Well, all right, get out! Nobody wants you around here anyway! But don't you try to make trouble for hard-working people, don't you dare try it! You hear me, old man?"

Mr. Nicholas had recovered his balance, with the aid of the bread stand, which was rather shaky.

He said breathlessly, "The trouble has already been made, by your husband. I advise you not to—"

"You advise me!" Her voice went up to a low shriek. "Don't you dare stand there and tell me what to do! Who do you think is going to listen to you—a useless old man that can't even take care of himself—that can't even see! And you come in here and tell me filthy lies about my husband—and that filthy girl, that dirty kid—!"

She burst into dry sobs—to Mr. Nicholas's relief. He had been trying to brace himself for an attack that would land him on the floor.

He said uncertainly, "You had better talk this over with your husband, Mrs. Rudd. He is in trouble—and he would have been in much worse trouble if I had not happened to interfere. Your husband is a dangerously ill man. He came very near to destroying a little girl the other night."

"Myra, Myra—don't listen to him! It's not true!"

Rudd, eager with despair, came half running toward them. His wife had fallen quiet, checking her sobs, listening.

"Myra, listen—nothing happened, he's lying—listen, wouldn't the kid have said something? Wasn't her father in here today—yesterday—wasn't he just like always? He's lying, Myra—he's lying!"

She said in a new voice, dulled and savage: "Tell me what happened, Will. You took that girl in his house? At night?"

"No! I never did! She went in by herself, Myra—by herself—I only tried to get her out so—"

"You followed her in? And the old man followed you?"

"No! I didn't! I mean, I don't know what he—"

"Wait," she said: a command. Then her dulled voice turned to Mr. Nicholas. "You tell me what you've got to say about my husband. Right now. Quick!"

"Myra—"

"Shut up!"

Mr. Nicholas hesitated. He saw no use in saying more to her than he had said. On the other hand, she was in no state to be refused. In his slight pausing, she seized his arm and shook it. Hysteria lay beneath a very thin control.

"Tell me!"

"I intend to," Mr. Nicholas said hastily. He did not try to alter or soften the facts he had already related—to Bud, to Dr. Linen—but simply began to relate them once more.

He had just begun, when someone came and rapped sharply on the door. To his wearied, sickened mind, hope came that this was the doctor; and with a sigh, he fell silent. Neither Rudd spoke. When the rapping came again, harder, Mrs. Rudd turned to her husband.

"Take him in back," she ordered, low.

"That is probably Dr. Linen," Mr. Nicholas said.

A Friend of Mary Rose

She went directly to the door, an act of courage he had not expected, and said sharply: "Who is it?"

The answer was indistinguishable to Mr. Nicholas, but it was not his friend's voice; he could tell that before she answered.

"No, we're closed early tonight. We're closed!"

Her husband hissed at her: *"Because of sickness!"* But she disdained this cue, and returned in hard silence. Passed them by.

"Bring him back here," she said, passing.

As he obeyed orders, Rudd's confusion vanished. He seized Mr. Nicholas's arm and began, as if he were a sack of potatoes, to haul him away.

If Mr. Nicholas could have got his stick free, he would have struck at him—but his wretched legs made this impossible. Made it all he could do, in fact, to keep upright on his journey. Grimly silent, he allowed himself to be hustled along. A heavy curtain brushed his face, and then he was past it and allowed to stand still. Rudd's dutiful hand still grasped his arm.

"Myra, don't let him—"

"Don't talk, let me hear. Go on," she ordered Mr. Nicholas. "You said the door was locked."

Mr. Nicholas went on. It seemed impossible to him that she should hear what her husband had done—what he was capable of doing—without collapsing in horror. He waited every moment for her to stop him, to say: "No more!" or simply to cry.

She did none of these things. From her silence, one could not guess that she was learning anything—or hearing anything. It was Rudd who found the recital unbearable to hear—who dropped Mr. Nicholas's arm and went into restless wandering, a peripheral protest that was all he dared make. Even when Mr. Nicholas had finished, he did not speak.

It was his wife who spoke to him.

"All right," she said, flat-voiced. "I told you. I told you you'd get into trouble with those rotten kids—you and your candy! I know what went on behind that counter! But that Hayden slut wasn't so easy, was she? What did you have to give her to get her into that house? What? Money?"

"I think your mind must be as diseased as your husband's!" said Mr. Nicholas.

She paid no attention. Neither to him nor to her husband's unhappy protests.

Her voice sharpened. She said, "And why didn't she say anything? Are you sure she didn't?"

The telephone rang, startling Rudd so badly that he knocked over some heavy pile of goods. A hand instantly took Mr. Nicholas's arm—a smaller, harder hand than Rudd's.

"Let it ring," said Mrs. Rudd.

They let it ring.

In the following silence she said thoughtfully, "No. She wouldn't dare say a word, that one. She knows better. And you should have known better, too, old man! Do you know how long we've worked to keep this store? How hard we've worked? Do you think I'm going to let you come in here and ruin us, at our age, on account of some rotten brat that ought to be in a detention home anyway?"

Mr. Nicholas said earnestly, "If it's not this child, it will be another. Your husband is out of control, Mrs. Rudd."

"Oh, no, he's not. I can control my husband." And as if in proof—triumphant proof—she said crisply into the room: "All right, Rudd. You got us into this, now do what I say and I'll get you out. He'll have to go down the cellar steps."

Rudd said humbly, "I don't know what you mean, Myra."

"Yes, you do. He had to go to the toilet. He asked to use the toilet. Then he fell down the steps."

She allowed them a brief silence.

Mr. Nicholas cried out: "Are you mad? God help you —do you mean to become *murderers?*"

Rudd blurted, "You keep still." He didn't move.

His wife said rapidly, "The doctor doesn't know, or he wouldn't have left him here. The girl's too scared to talk. It's only him, Rudd. Just him."

Rudd didn't answer. But in his farther part of the room he stirred, began to come forward. A door near Mr. Nicholas was flung open, a light switch snapped.

He exclaimed, "But what are you thinking? Don't you realize you are—"

"You shut up, old man," Rudd said softly. "You ought to been dead a long time anyway."

He was coming up behind Mr. Nicholas, who suddenly swung round, raking air with his rising stick as he turned.

Elizabeth Fenwick

It was an instinctive movement, the movement of a much younger man—and it cost him his balance. But that loss of balance, the glancing stagger against Rudd, somehow entangled them with the partition curtain—and caught Rudd's reaching hands in the curtain as well.

Mr. Nicholas staggered past. He did not fall. He did not know where he was at all, and could not think for sheer horror. He knew he had no hope of reaching the front of the store, and that his voice would not carry from here to the street.

Nevertheless, with all his might, he shouted for help—and shouting, grasped at whatever he could reach, with both hands—letting his stick fall—and threw these objects as hard as he could toward the front. One of them—a can of something—crashed dully against the blinded glass. Then he was seized, and his mouth covered by Rudd's large hand.

Rudd was almost weeping with rage and fear.

"Shut up, shut up, shut up . . ." he gibbered, over and over.

Mr. Nicholas flung himself violently left and right, Rudd swaying behind him, struggling to enforce his grip. He was hampered by the need to cover that shouting mouth, still making muffled calls into his hand.

"Myra, *Myra*—!"

She was there, too, a vicious and silent attacker, not what he needed at all.

"Hold him. . . ."

One of Mr. Nicholas's arms flailed free, and instantaneously the hand grasped and flung another can. This one hit some pile of goods, or fragile display, and the entire structure toppled and crashed in echoing reverberations.

Above these echoes, a louder thundering came upon the front door, and a shouting that was perfectly clear to the wordless, struggling three within.

"Open this door! Open this door!"

It was Linen.

With something—perhaps his foot—he broke glass. Instantly Rudd dropped his prisoner and turned and ran.

Mr. Nicholas, catching at shelving to keep from falling, half falling against a counter and gripping that, was still aware that Rudd did not run far. His wife, crying out shrilly, had caught up with him and would not let him go. At the front of the store, a shouting Linen was knocking out more glass, and Mr. Nicholas continued breathlessly to call to him.

But Mrs. Rudd screamed louder than all these sounds, as if oblivious to them all.

"No, Will—no! Don't leave me—don't—"

"Let *go!*"

From Rudd, there was only the one hard snarl. Then abruptly, scuffle and scream broke off together. There was a moment of some violent suspension; and then began a gagging, retching sound that choked off Mr. Nicholas's own voice. Rudd had the woman by the throat—trying to choke her loose from him as he had done to Mr. Nicholas. And there was no way to stop him—if he left the counter, Mr. Nicholas knew that he would fall. He could only cling, and hear, and his faint, exhausted attempts to cry out were lost in the doctor's shouts and smashing of glass.

The front door slammed open. The ghastly noises stopped. Rudd was running. Some back door was torn violently open and his running footsteps pounded beyond it—away, out of hearing. It was the doctor's running steps he heard now, coming toward him—and knowing this, Mr. Nicholas sagged forward, with his whirling head on the cash register.

Chapter Fifteen

"I don't think it was a thing the man could ever have done, consciously," Dr. Linen said. "Killing that damned woman, I mean. He certainly must have hated her like the devil, and yet he's absolutely lost without her."

With the moral superiority of a man wearing his clothes, and free to walk in and out, he gave this opinion down to his friend lying in bed.

Mr. Nicholas murmured, "It may be as he says, that he didn't mean to do it."

"Well, his hands meant to do it, whatever he says—or thinks. You don't get that much damage from halfhearted squeezing. And he certainly wasn't hesitating much about pushing you down those steps! No, I had that man pegged all along, John. All along. A very violent type, potentially."

Mr. Nicholas forbore pointing out that a little advance pegging would have been welcome, in this case; and as if scenting forbearance, the doctor added: "What threw me off—or never put me on—was the little-girl business.

I certainly never heard anything like that about him, and apparently he had no previous record at all. But I told you that."

"Perhaps that poor miserable wife of his protected him."

"Maybe. But it's a tricky business, this child-molestation. The children themselves are often hesitant to say anything, out of a vague feeling they've done something wrong, too. And too many parents, if they do find out, regard it as some kind of disgrace, and keep quiet about it. If no violence has occurred to the child—which was apparently the case here. Often the father will go over and settle it himself, especially in a neighborhood like ours, where people are leery of the police in general. But I never even saw him in bad shape—certainly never patched him up. He had some dandy scratches on his arms, by the way," he added. "Your little friend must never cut her nails."

"You did go talk to Bud, didn't you?" said Mr. Nicholas.

He turned his head anxiously on the pillow, toward his friend's face.

"I did, I told you I did. And it was a waste of time—everybody on DeKuyper Street knew last night that I broke in and caught Rudd strangling his wife. The latest version is that I also pursued and caught him—I don't know what all the police cars were supposed to be for. Background music, maybe. You don't figure in the legend at all, you know," he said cheerfully. "It's all brave me."

A Friend of Mary Rose

"Well, actually it *was*, Roger. If you hadn't come . . ."

"What did you expect me to do, when they wouldn't answer their damned telephone? I was worried about you! And then to find the place shut up and dark . . . Do you know what I thought at first?"

"What?" said Mr. Nicholas, obligingly.

"I thought you'd spotted the fellow, and got Rudd to come after him with you! I could just see you hobbling down some dark street, dragging Rudd along, and some devil waiting with a blackjack for you both! No, really," he said, drowning his patient's faint laugh with his own much heartier one. "What else could I think? It's exactly the kind of thing you'd do, and I knew it—and I was standing there cussing you out—and myself—when all of a sudden the ceiling fell down inside. And then I noticed the cracked door, of course. And began improving on it a bit."

He was enjoying himself enormously, no one could doubt it. Mr. Nicholas, who was not, didn't begrudge him his pleasure. He was glad not to be a total Jonah to everyone who offered him hospitality—first Lettie, now Roger. And Mrs. Linen had been noble about receiving him back into her house, in spite of the forbidden excitements he got her husband involved in. She was also coping with Dorothea, he understood; he didn't dare to inquire how.

He really felt quite subdued this morning, and not inclined to inquire about anything. It rather surprised him that the doctor—the great subduer—should not notice this, and should go on sitting there and roaring at him in this way. Mr. Nicholas, both guest and patient, could only respond politely, and endure.

Perhaps his endurance began to show, for Dr. Linen got up.

He said reluctantly, "Well, I'll get out of here now and let you rest. You may be indestructible—I think you are—but damn it, you're still mortal. And eighty-five!"

"Eighty-three," Mr. Nicholas corrected.

"Oh, is that all? Well, I told your people they could see you this evening, but your little girl friend and her handsome brother are going to have to wait another day or so. Lord, the men certainly have the looks in that family! Even the father's not bad-looking, you know, now that Mrs. Reilly's got him cleaned up. I think she's rather got her eye on him, too."

A faint, familiar twinge of anxiety touched at Mr. Nicholas. In spite of himself, he murmured: "Isn't Mary Rose pretty at all?"

The moment he said this, he was so cross with himself that he turned his head away, deliberately shut out the doctor's tactful reply. What earthly difference did it make? And what could he do about it, if she wasn't?

Nothing. His brief responsibility for Mary Rose was over, and he was glad it was over. It had been too much for him in the first place.

Besides, all girls were pretty, once they got old enough to do something about it.

Alone in his room once more, he relaxed, turning his head back toward the open window. Calm air floated in to him the familiar sounds of his old neighborhood. It was not DeKuyper Street, but it might have been; the same busy echoes were washing round his old house not far away, although it stood closed against them, and empty (except for the dining-room furniture).

The house was empty in his mind, too. All that he cared for was out of it, and his long life of responsibility there was ended. It had really ended long ago, he knew; that little girl—that unexpected little girl—had been his first real responsibility in many years. No doubt she would be his last. Perhaps that was why his tired mind still clung to the idea of her. She was, for him, the essence of all that would not come again: the anxieties, the necessities, the painful care. The love.

He really did not want any more of it. What he wanted now was his room and his cat and his trunks. The ordinary sounds of Dorrie, going about the house. His in-and-out Boy and Girl. Johnny, laughing.

But he would have one unexpected last treasure for his trunk, now. That box, with its smooth stones and peeled twigs, its poker chip and marbles and bit of chamois, and that plastic or celluloid object he still couldn't make out. . . .

What *was* the confounded thing, anyway?

Well, it didn't matter. He was too tired to care.

On the other hand, the box was right beside his bed. To make sure of this, he reached out and found it. Then he took off the lid and found the plastic thing, baffling as ever.

He sighed, and took it out for another try.

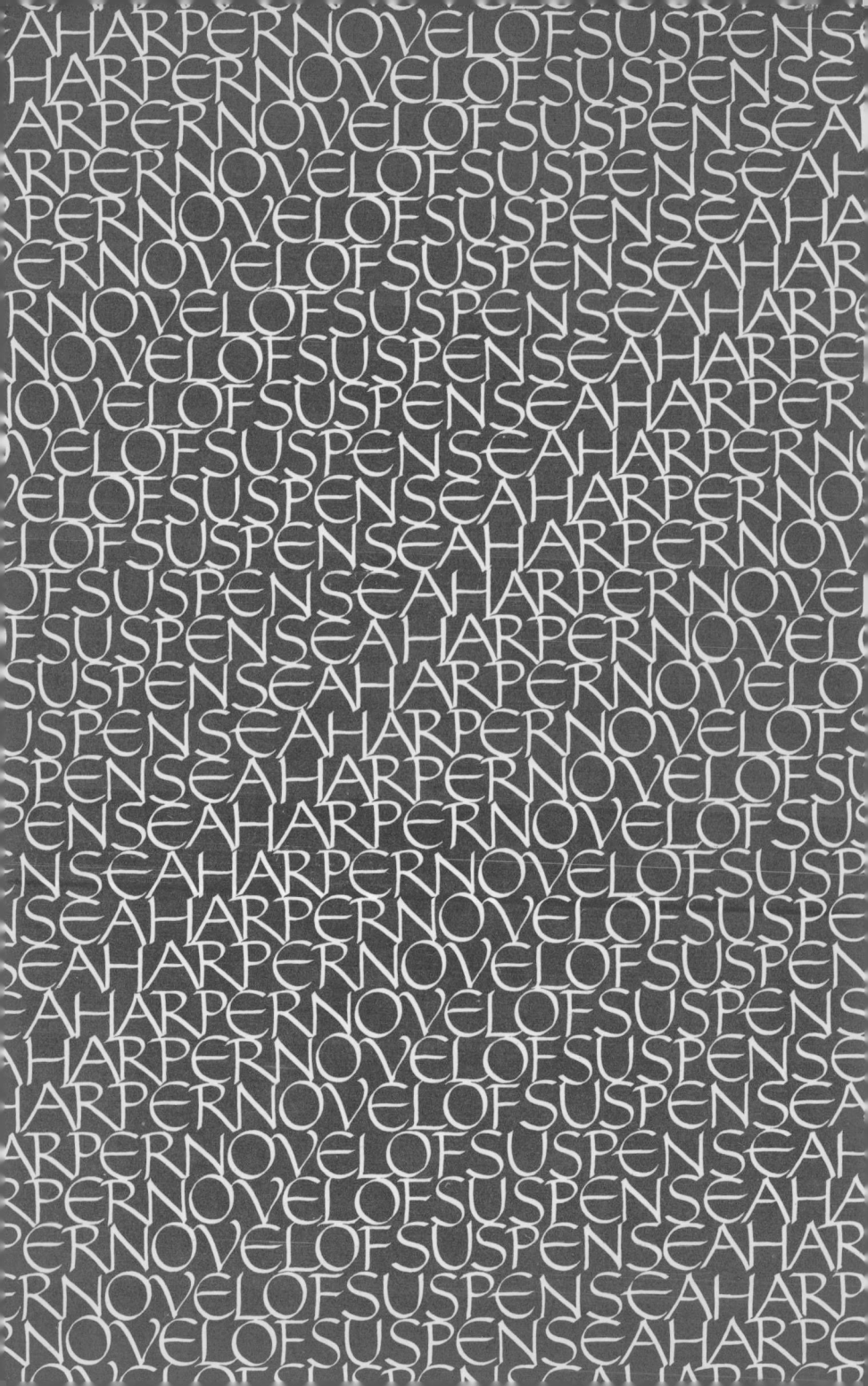